Light
between the Leaves

MOLLY G. SHANE

iUniverse, Inc.
Bloomington

Light between the Leaves

Copyright © 2011 by Molly G. Shane

All rights reserved. No part of this book may be used or reproduced by any means, graphic, electronic, or mechanical, including photocopying, recording, taping or by any information storage retrieval system without the written permission of the publisher except in the case of brief quotations embodied in critical articles and reviews.

iUniverse books may be ordered through booksellers or by contacting:

iUniverse
1663 Liberty Drive
Bloomington, IN 47403
www.iuniverse.com
1-800-Authors (1-800-288-4677)

Because of the dynamic nature of the Internet, any web addresses or links contained in this book may have changed since publication and may no longer be valid. The views expressed in this work are solely those of the author and do not necessarily reflect the views of the publisher, and the publisher hereby disclaims any responsibility for them.

Any people depicted in stock imagery provided by Thinkstock are models, and such images are being used for illustrative purposes only.

Certain stock imagery © Thinkstock.

ISBN: 978-1-4620-2628-9 (sc)
ISBN: 978-1-4620-2629-6 (e)

Printed in the United States of America

iUniverse rev. date: 08/30/2011

Introduction

My purpose in writing Christian fiction is to show the depth of God's facets, bear witness to the unbelievers, and assist in others' continued Christian development. We are a part of the largest kingdom!

My hope is for readers to gain a stronger relationship with Him through the examples of my characters. I have learned to listen and ask Him to lead me, and lead He does! I cannot count the number of times I have gone before Him in prayer, to open the Bible and be guided to a message that contained the answers to my questions—not always the answers I want, mind you. Through that delicate relationship, He continues to teach me, and I will continue to sprout from a seed into a fruitful spirit, through Him.

I interwove fact and fiction, not only to create an entertaining escape but also to help readers learn about our God and our world. Each book I write, I gain knowledge. The biggest impact I felt from writing *Light between the Leaves* was discovering an entire expanse of life in the ocean I had never known before. How isolated the northwest Hawaiian region is, yet how large an affect we have on it.

If we glance down our street, what would we see that afflicts our health and well being? If items we buy, consume, and throw away affects plants and animals in remote parts of our earth, imagine what they are doing to us right here. I can proudly say I recycle, but there is always more I can learn and do.

How could I not write about scuba diving? I was awestruck as a whole new world opened to me when I received my NAUI certification and leapt into the big blue for the first time! The explorations gave me a higher level of respect for the Creator. We only experience a speck of the universe. I have performed a copious part of my research with the findings from NOAA (the National Oceanic Atmospheric Administration). Take some time to visit their website.

Every time I dive, I uncover something unique. I'll never forget the time my husband and I were separated from a dive group and ended up in a desert of sorts. I prayed and asked God to wow me with some wild creature. A batfish glided nonchalantly across our path. It was one of the strangest creatures I have ever seen.

Yes, we must work hard to make a living, and in return we gain worth and dignity. God also intends for us to enjoy the playgrounds He made. Next time you are outside, intensely observe a leaf or pay attention to the wonderful diversity of people at the store. He could have made us all the same. We are to rejoice in the unique. Thank you, God!

I give glory to God for this book. Yes, I came up with the ideas, poured my heart into the plot, character development, and research, and wrote this novel. He is the one who gave me the ability. Of my free will, I asked the Lord to lead me in its construction.

Why Christian sci-fi? I find it fascinating to think creatively about things we can merely speculate on. Christian sci-fi also provides an alternative source of fun in a Christian light.

The appendix contains a study of the fruits and gifts of the Holy Spirit, a glossary, and suggested lesson plans with a template. Teachers hold a special place in my heart with their countless acts of selfless dedication and time to further their education and ours. They will find the lesson plans useful as they lead others in study.

The section on spiritual fruits and gifts was included in response to the continual growth of our relationship with God. It explains ways to talk, hear, and listen to Him. It is important to know how He has blessed each one of us, and in what manner, so we can use those spiritual gifts to improve the world He brought into existence.

One of the great things about this novel is the ability to get a book club started and be able to discuss the scriptures within. By request, I will call in during your meeting, and we can talk about it. Visit my website at mollygshane.com for more details on how to schedule this. There is also a fan page on Facebook.com to keep you updated!

Here is to you, the reader, the supporter of Christian works. I am thankful He created YOU. Hugs and blessings as you grow. Stretch yourself.

In Christ's Love,

Molly G. Shane

Chapter 1

Estaline Cassell pawed a fallen lock of hair with the back of her hand. Soil, dark as molasses, stuck under her short finger nails and smeared across her palms. The cool, moist dirt gathered in soft crumbles. A fusion of sweet scents coalesced in light undertones. She grabbed the pink garden gloves laid over an orchid crate.

Rivala Public Gardens were maintained by a throng of volunteers. College students came to work in exchange for class credits. Essa had cultivated, planted, and maintained the grounds for three years.

She gazed upward along the layers of meshed bark on an orange crownshaft palm and admired its beauty. How could she ever think about leaving? She knew someone needed to teach the human race the effects of deforestation and steps to reduce harmful chemicals that killed the plant life. There was more of this beauty to save in the wild. If only others knew the delicate connection it had to our vitality.

So many people had come through Rivala's doors, having no idea how to care for the plants around them, let alone how to conserve them. Visitors walked along the flagstone paths glued together by fuzzy pillow moss. Candy bar wrappers and tissues showed where they had been. She had seen a lady turn her back to answer her cell phone as her kids climbed over the short stone wall into the gardens. Essa needed to be a change agent.

Before college graduation, she had piled through line after line of open jobs on the computer at her grandma's house. Few were available worldwide in her career field. One position was in the basement of some testing facility; another was for field research on cacti in the desert. Finally, after months of searching, it popped up across the screen: Professor of Botany at the University of Hawaii.

Had she gone to heaven? More importantly, had she flipped her lid? The assignment was thousands of miles away. Something was bound to come up where she currently lived, right? Reality hit, and she realized the job would be gone in a heartbeat. It wouldn't hurt to apply. That opportunity wouldn't come again. Who was to say she would even get a call back. She had filled out the application, shrugged, hit "apply," and put it out of her mind.

She kneeled on a foam pad in her mucked-up jean shorts and yellow faded short-sleeve shirt with green trim. She took her time pruning back a rainbow shower tree and plucked the weeds around it. It was one of her favorite species. The blooms hung in cascades of hues from peach to blushed orange. Only a portion of her calves and feet were visible from under the foliage.

She felt a tap on the sole of her shoe and chucked it up to a kid passing by. She pulled back to grab her organic disease prevention spray. The thick legged receptionist stood next to her and bent down.

"This came for you." She handed Essa a cream-colored envelope. The words were neatly type written, "University of Hawaii at Manoa."

Essa sat on the foam board and crossed her legs. She stared at the envelope while rubbing her shaky hands on a rag. It was thin, like a rejection letter. If it were an offer, surely it would be thick with forms. She glanced both ways down the path before leaning back under the bush to read it.

She couldn't bring herself to open the seal. What do I do when I don't have a clue what *to* do? Prayer snapped into her mind. "*Dear Father, help me deal with whatever news this is. Retain my confidence and strength if it's a denial. Lord, You gave me wonderful tools and didn't create me to just sit and watch the world go by. Help find a position in life You'd be proud to have me do. I promise to fulfill Your desires. In Jesus' name, Amen.*"

"There you are!" Mason must have recognized her dirty yellow tennis shoes. He grabbed her by the ankles and pulled her to him.

She shoved the letter into her back pocket. He knew she'd been looking for jobs, but she hadn't told him she found an opportunity in Hawaii and applied for it. "Hey, you!" Her face tightened.

Mason held her sweaty face in his hands and planted a kiss on her lips. "Are you ready for lunch?"

"Yeah, I'll go clean up in the wash room." Standing, she swiped her hands together to dust the crumbs of soil from her skin. "Where are we going?"

"I figured you'd be . . ." He stopped and looked her over. "In a bit of disarray, so I thought we'd get a bite here in the café."

She was really looking at getting her mouth around a juicy burger, but being in a botanical garden, the café capitalized on the vegan side. A dry veggie patty didn't seem to cut it. "I only have a twenty-minute break. If we drove somewhere, I'd probably end up with only five minutes to eat," she conceded.

In the café, they took their food and sat at a wrought-iron, two-seated table. She wiggled and attempted to get comfortable.

"Heard back from any jobs you've applied for?"

"No calls or e-mails." She replied. Why even mention Hawaii when it was most likely a "thanks, but" correspondence.

She took a large bite of her salad and hoped he wouldn't ask any more questions. He changed the topic, and they spent the rest of lunch talking about unrelated subjects. Lunch ended, and she gave Mason a peck on the cheek.

Essa went to the tool closet and added a spade and spray bottle to her belt. She maneuvered around the on-lookers in the dome and returned to her list of duties.

Chapter 2

"I have to go." Essa's voice cracked, and tears threatened to pour from her almond-shaped eyes.

Her best friend, Willa, sat beside her on the bench in front of their old apartment. The spring breeze had a bite. She pulled her dark-brown pea coat around her shoulders. "Not many people get job offers right after they graduate, especially in Hawaii," Willa said. She threw her arms up in excitement, and her springy blonde curls bounced. "Won't you regret leaving everything behind?" she asked in her high-pitched voice. Willa had often been mistaken for being younger than she was, with reason. "There are not a whole lot of jobs out there in botany," Willa continued. "Don't you see the perks–for you?"

Essa realized she was one of the lucky graduates. She had received the teaching position at the University of Hawaii and was excited to lecture on the botany, historical symbolism, and medicinal purposes.

They stared at the giggling group of new college students moving into their former unit. Willa shook her head and nodded toward them. "All I can see is a vast group of strangers out there who don't share the crazy humor that you and I do."

Essa related to Willa's anxiety at finding new friends.

"AHHH!" A student with ponytails all over his head ran past and stuck out his tongue at some passing girls.

Willa tilted her head towards him. "What am I supposed to do, befriend the immature?"

"Jesus would," Essa said, chuckling.

Willa turned her freckled face toward Essa. "Think about the big hole you'll leave in your family. It's not like you'll be ten miles down the road anymore."

"I find it interesting that you haven't mentioned my boyfriend as a reason to stay."

"Eh? He's . . . whatever. Think about your grandma," Willa said.

Essa rolled her eyes. "My grandma is the one encouraging me. Yes, she's sad, but she understands."

Essa had moved in with her Grandma Rose after graduation and while looking for a job. It made sense, seeing that grandma needed help taking her medication, doing lawn work, and just managing everyday chores. One of her favorite moments was right before her grandma would take a nap.

They'd lie across Rose's bed and look out the open window at the neighbors walking by. Essa loved the feel of wrapping her fingers around the chenille petals sewn on the blanket. The warm caresses from the breeze calmed her.

Essa thought of one recent afternoon when she and Rose were gazing out the same window, as usual. Essa laid her head on her crossed arms.

Grandma rubbed her eyes. "I expect the world could use your knowledge. We need it to stay beautiful."

"It's not as pretty as it once was. The gases released into the atmosphere create a photochemical smog, and the plants do not get the light needed. It disrupts the complex balance that supports life." Essa sighed and stared at the ceiling. "I want to educate people on how this happens and what they can do to change it."

"I will be proud to see you lead the world to a better future and get the opportunity to spread those wings, I mean leaves." Rose laughed at her own joke.

Essa leaned her head on her grandma's shoulder. "Jobs are hard to find, but I'm thankful we get to spend this time together."

Willa broke into Essa's thoughts with a touch on the arm, bringing her back to the present.

"You're going to miss them, aren't you?" Willa asked.

"My whole family knew that I would eventually be moving on."

Willa tilted her head. "Who will take care of Rose?"

"My brother, I guess."

"Not Camille?"

Essa's brother, Blaise, was married to a high-profile lawyer. He had been laid off the previous year, and they decided to try for children. They both agreed he would check in on Rose. Her younger sister, Camille, on the other hand, was always chasing odd jobs around the country. Her latest was as a white-water rafting guide in the mountains of Tennessee.

"Camille calls my parents about once a month. Mom tells me where she is and what she is doing. There seems to be a special connection between her and Grandma Rose. She receives letters from her about once a week, but I've never read them. I figure if Camille wants me to know about her life or wonders how I am, she'll send me one, too."

Willa had only seen Essa's sister a handful of times. Camille was usually occupied with her group of friends or a new passion. "It baffles me how two people can grow up together just to grow apart."

"Our personalities are polar opposites. We've always been interested in different things. At least Blaise and I have the same view the majority of the time."

Willa twitched a knowing smile. She had had a crush on Blaise throughout high school, but, then again, every girl did. She clasped her hands together. "As a last ditch effort, let's bring up the boy toy."

"He is *not* a boy toy. My gosh, Willa, how was I supposed to know I would not fall in love with him? No one knows that kind of thing."

"Even so, what are you gonna tell him?"

"The truth."

Willa threw her head to the side and made a guttural sound.

"I leave in one week to get settled in." Essa paused before continuing. "Will you come for a few days and help me?"

Willa stared at her blankly. "I–I would love to, but it costs so much to get out there. Plus all the time I would have to take off work and find a replacement."

"You've always been the oh-so-rational one. You took cosmetology classes in high school and started working right after graduation. You own a popular studio with ten employees. I get it. If you don't want to, just tell me."

"Let me think about it, okay?" Willa wasn't sure whether she wanted to say goodbye to her friend twice.

Essa looked down at her watch. "It's time I go meet Mason at the flower shop. He suggested we pick something out for my grandma's birthday."

"When are you going to tell him?"

"I've been avoiding it up till now. It has to be today, or it may never happen."

Essa gave Willa a hug and walked back to her '86 AMC Eagle holed with rust. She had purchased it with cash, and it ran the four years she needed it to while in college. She adjusted her mirror with care and moved the seat back a touch. She became aware of what she was doing. There I go again, stalling, she thought. The last thing she wanted to do was break Mason's heart.

She adjusted the gears and turned into the street. He was a great Christian and a wonderful boyfriend over the past year, but she knew he wasn't the *one*. He was five years her senior and already had an established position as a financial advisor. Mason even mentioned looking for land to build a house because he was tired of living in an apartment.

She pulled up to the flower shop. An array of colors showed through the large store front windows. Buds of yellow teardrops sprang from tall knobby shoots. Orange blooms the size of her hand lit up the middle.

Essa opened the glove box and got a mint. She lingered in her car until the mint dissolved in her mouth. Then she figured she should check her tires. Something might have gotten stuck in them on the drive over. It paid to be careful. When she couldn't delay any longer, she started towards the flower shop.

Mason met her in the doorway. He held it open and took her by the hand to a small table in the corner of the store.

A portly man sat opposite them, wearing a short white scarf around his neck. He smiled at them knowingly while he hoisted a book of floral photos for her to view.

She gave him a skeptical frown and opened the book. Each page boasted large arrangements. She turned to Mason. "I think these are just a *little* too big for Grandma's birthday and probably too expensive for my budget." She turned back to the man. "What else do you have?"

The man stared back at Mason.

Essa crumpled her brows. This was for *her* grandma. Maybe the man didn't know.

Mason lifted his index finger to the florist and got up from his chair. He offered a hand to Essa and guided her in front of a black iron arbor displaying potted roses on each side. The vines skirted up and around the cross beams. Wild ferns created a half circle behind them in massive tiered levels. She noticed lady slippers flowers, intermixed in delicate purples.

Mason took her other hand in his and shifted her attention

back to him. A toothy smile spread across his mouth. He let go of one hand and dug in his pocket.

Essa suddenly connected everything together.

"Oh, no, no!" she shouted. She had to stop this immediately. The little strings that made up her life began to unravel, dropping one-by-one. There was no way to explain why she hadn't told him she was leaving before this moment. "I can't marry you!"

The florist actually shrieked from the corner, surprised at her sudden outburst.

Everything stopped. Mason's jaw dropped, and the customers' eyes focused on her. Mason looked at her face, confused, and then opened his hand to reveal a tiny pin.

She glanced down at the pin, and her breath escaped her in a rush. Her face got hot, then hotter when she realized what a scene she had just made. She lifted her eyes to his with a crooked smile.

He shook his head in slow motion. "This is for your grandma." He wiped the sweat beginning to form on his forehead. "Don't worry about me asking you to marry me. If I had any intention of asking you, I don't now."

His words hit her like a bull dozer. A prickly sensation heated her cheeks. Words escaped her, and she had nowhere to run. She stood in frozen isolation. The customers went back to what they were doing. The florist waddled over with a chair and an oriental hand fan. She raised her arm to disregard it.

Essa managed to collect her car keys and walked robot-like out of the door. She glanced back at Mason, who watched her from the store window. His face had turned the color of chalk and was etched with desperation. She took a deep breath, collected herself, and peeled out of the parking lot.

Essa tore open the folding doors of her closet and rummaged for a jacket. The spring weather still held a chill at night.

She thought about the confrontation in the flower shop. *It's better I told Mason now than make him wait. Who am I to string* a man along for years? She let out a long breath. He'll be better off and can now search for a girl who will appreciate him.

Her attempt at self-justification was hollow. A gnawing in her stomach twisted and churned. *How am I ever going find the right man if I keep picking ones whom I'm not in love with?* Mason was a gentleman, which was hard to find, and always called her at night to see how her day had gone. Whenever she had a hard day and spoke harshly to him, he always realized it and stroked her arms to calm her. *What if I'm making a mistake? What if he is the best one out there and I just screwed it up? Affections can grow over time.*

The phone rang, and she almost didn't pick it up. She heard Willa's voice on the other line. She wanted to know what had happened with Mason, and Essa gave her a summary.

"I'm still coming to youth group tonight," Essa told her. She needed a diversion.

"I wasn't sure if you'd want to spend quiet time alone with God or with us. The conversation with Mason sounds like it was hard. How did he take it?"

She didn't want to admit she felt as if she had misread their entire relationship. "I'll tell you all the bitter details when I get there," Essa promised.

She pinned the layers of her cascading caramel hair into a twist on top of her head, kissed her grandma on the cheek, and scooted out the door.

Tonight she would meet with her Bible study group for the last time. *How will I possibly find a church where I fit in so well,* she wondered. *I won't know anyone and will be too afraid to sing praise in front of strangers.*

Essa sidled through the crowd in the hallway and gave the occasional wave. She had been dedicated at this church and had grown up with the families. Some came and left, but for the most part, these relationships had become a sturdy, though complex, support beam. They had become a part of her identity.

She had taken classes that added to her spiritual and religious growth. One in particular taught her how to recognize her personal strengths and weaknesses. She identified one of her flaws as needing to spend more time developing her one-on-one relationship with God. Essa had no idea how to even go about communicating *with* Him. On the opposite pendulum, her greatest strength was faith, simple, strong, and true.

She walked through the door and noticed that all the chairs in the classroom were arranged in a circle, as usual, but a long table was set up with piles of finger foods and sodas.

"Surprise!" her fellow classmates and Vati, her Bible study leader, exclaimed.

Essa's eyes opened wide, and her mouth hung open. "You're so sneaky. Willa, did you know about this?"

"Not at all," Willa said, grinning sarcastically.

She tilted her head and gazed at the ceiling in an attempt to block the growing tears. "This change has been more difficult than I expected. It's so hard to leave everything and *everyone* to head in a direction I've never gone before."

"Great people will come into your life," one of her classmates said.

"Probably," Essa's voice cracked. "But they won't be any of you."

"Having the same friends all the time is boring!" Willa said, sniffling.

Vati placed her hands on Essa's shoulders. "We're going to miss you." She raised her thick, black brows. "You must keep in touch so we can follow along with your adventures."

One girl asked, "Does this mean we're not having a study tonight?"

"No," Vati answered, "but it does mean you should get over to the table and grab some food!"

A few minutes after everyone settled in their seats, Vati took hers, as well, and opened to a page of her Bible. "I had this material pre-decided last fall. Listen to what God would like you to hear from this lesson and may call your attention to. This form of communication is called *rhema*." She explained, "Our spirit recognizes when God is speaking directly to it via scripture. It usually pertains to an existing situation or it may guide you in the future. Each of us may get something different from one scripture."

Essa prayed for God to lead her and remembered He did not put a fear in her heart. That was a struggle she was trying to evade. I feel so lost, she thought. I've tried in desperation to call out to God and hear Him but get nothing. I must be missing how to receive His messages and signs because other people seem to. She blew a strand of layered hair out of her face.

"Let's go in prayer." Vati nodded to a guy to Essa's right. Essa tapped her foot.

He began to pray. "Father, we praise Your name and lift it up. May we reflect Your image You've created us to be. Grant us understanding of what You would have us do and walk side-by-side along our paths. In Jesus' name, amen."

They opened their eyes, and Essa raised her hand. She was about to speak, then hesitated.

Vati's warm, black eyes softened in an accepting manner.

Essa gazed back and forth at her friends, while biting her lower lip. "I would *love* to hear from God or be able to get a personal message from Him." She paused and shook her head. "But I don't. I–I just wonder if *I'm* doing something wrong. I refuse to believe He created people only to put a huge space between Him and us where we cannot access Him."

Vati took her hand. "You're not alone. This troubles so many. The problem has to do with our culture and the constant zoom of things around us. Think of the continual noise, like the radio, TV, movies, people talking, work, and class. How are we supposed to focus on God when all those things are competing for our attention?"

Vati stood up and walked around the room. "God does not need to come to us. He is already here—everywhere. He gives *us* the choice, out of free will, if or when we search for Him."

"But how?" Essa was eager to connect with her Heavenly

Father. She desired in a secret place in her soul that God had made her for something great.

"One way is through rhema words in scripture. Another is by signs. It is a general rule that if you feel confused by what you have experienced, it is not from God. He clarifies things and puts a peace in your soul. This may take some practice but will eventually become natural." Vati pointed at her. "You watch, Essa. I've got a feeling that He has something special for *you*."

Essa wasn't sure if she understood but felt willing to give it a chance.

Vati looked around the group. "The word 'beginning' is referenced back to Genesis in the Bible. Let's look at another metaphor for beginning." She ran along the text with her index finger before finding the right place on the page. "God prepares us for life and the journeys we'll take with gifts of the spirit and guidance. Luke chapter eight, verses ten through fifteen, talks about a seed and how it can grow."

Essa wondered whether all the talk about beginnings had something to do with her.

Vati reached behind her back, grabbed her long black braid, and placed it in front of one shoulder. "Justin, can you please read verse ten?"

" 'The knowledge of the secrets of the kingdom of God has been given to you, but to others I speak in parables, so that, through seeing, they may not see; though hearing, they may not understand.' " His deep voice echoed a strong presence.

God knows my entire life ahead, Essa thought. "It is already written," she remembered from a previous study. Courage rose in her soul, and she gave thanks for the affirmation to move on to the next stage in her life. The seed could be an analogy for the initial launch into the unknown. She realized that this idea could make a great base to incorporate into her teaching.

"Continuing in Luke, chapter eight, verses eleven through fifteen." Vati lowered her voice to a whisper. " 'This is the meaning of the parable: the seed is the Word of God.' "

Light between the Leaves

A seed! Essa thought. He is talking to me about things I am so familiar with. She leaned forward with her chin on her hand.

Vati continued. " 'Those along the path are the ones who hear. The devil attempts to come and take away the Word from our hearts, so that they may not believe and be saved.' "

Essa recalled the devil being described as a thief in the night and the on-going spiritual warfare between Christians and the wicked.

" 'Those on the rock are the ones who receive the word with joy when they hear it, but they have no root. They believe for awhile, but in the time of testing they fall away. The seed that fell among thorns stands for those who hear, but as they go on their way they are choked by life's worries, riches and pleasures, and they do not mature.' "

I need to stop worrying. She took a deep breath. I've got to remove the burdens and give it to God, again and again."

" 'But the seed on good soil stands for those with a noble and good heart, who hear the Word, retain it, and by receiving, produce a crop.' " Vati finished the scripture.

After class ended and most of the students had gone, Essa approached Vati. "Is our pastor still here?"

"He left," Vati said, glancing at her watch, "but he should be in tomorrow morning."

Essa frowned. She could've used some insight into God's intentions for having her leave and what He may have in store for her. "I was hoping to talk with him."

Vati smiled. "He called a church in Hawaii close to where you'll be staying." She pulled a folded piece of paper and a little box from her bag. "Pastor Bob wanted me to give this to you before you left."

"Thank you." She started to open it.

Vati placed her hand over Essa's. "He asked that you wait to read it when you are on the plane."

Chapter 3

The scene at the airport was typical. Her mother wept on her Hawaiian button-down tee shirt that matched her father's. Blaise sported a dark tan that contrasted against his sandy blonde hair. His wife, Greta, wore her typical three-piece suit, and Grandma Rose attempted to lift their spirits. She danced her rendition of the hula. She pretended to be startled by her body's ability to wiggle. Essa's attempt at restraining her laughter resulted in an escaped snort, making her family howl louder. The only one missing was Camille, which wasn't a surprise. At least Willa had decided to go with her.

Rose lifted her saggy arms and placed her palms on Essa's high-boned cheeks. Her eyes drooped with a sad gaze. "You, my dear, were created for great things. Now, go do them."

"I will," Essa whispered the promise into the small space between them.

After passing through security and waiting to board, Essa filed her way through the crowded airplane. She compared her ticket to the empty row, heaved her brown and pink polka-dotted luggage case into the overhead bin, and sat in the middle of three seats. Willa had managed to relax in her seat several aisles down.

She closed her eyes and placed her hands together. "*Dear Lord, please seat a handsome guy next to me. Amen.*" She opened her eyes to see a tall twenty-something man with chiseled features standing in the aisle directly beside of her. Essa watched him fiddle with a stuck zipper on his suitcase.

He pulled at the zipper once more, his biceps popping, and threw his bag across the row of seats. It grazed her nose and landed on the cushion. She gasped in audible surprise.

He looked down at her and lifted the corner of his mouth. She was in **his** way. His legs pushed hers aside. He stood in her floor space and wrestled the suitcase into the leg area in front of his seat.

I guess I should've been more specific in my prayer, she thought.

She sighed and lifted herself with the balls of her feet to see whom Willa had ended up sitting next to. She spied her friend deep in conversation with a nun to her left and the sun streaming over her body from the window on her right. How did she get so blessed? Essa stole a peek at the rude man next to her–handsome, but rude.

How am I going to get through a four-hour flight with this guy? She contemplated asking the flight attendant if there was an empty seat to switch to, but couldn't bring herself to inquire in front of him.

She attempted to close her eyes once more and anticipated a peaceful, long nap. Her mind was racing and refused to stop. She felt her left arm jostle. A middle-aged woman had sat down. She smiled at Essa and extended her hand.

The lady barked a cough. "I'm Holly." She held up one finger and cleared the phlegm from her throat. "Off to Hollywood?" she asked.

Essa thought that was a strange question for her to be asking.

The flight was landing in San Francisco, not Los Angeles. She just shook her head, trying to discourage further discussion.

"I'm not either. So where are you going then?"

Essa leaned away from her, unfortunately putting her closer to the guy on the other side. "It's just a layover for me."

The woman went on and on, not even pausing when the captain's voice resonated over the loudspeaker, nor when the flight attendants explained procedures.

Her thoughts drifted off to questions. Was she doing the right thing by leaving? What if her life would have turned out better if she had stayed? Instead, she was giving up her best friend, boyfriend, and family. Whom would she celebrate the holidays with? She had figured once she had made the decision regarding the position, all concerns would disappear. Now there were more.

I won't be there to watch Blaise's children grow. How am I going to eradicate the guilt of leaving Grandma Rose? She needed to remind herself why she took this job in the first place; there was something more to life she was searching for. Her spirit stirred, and it wasn't just the storm beginning to form in the cool, electrified air enveloping the plane.

The next morning they boarded the flight from San Francisco to Oahu. The five-hour journey consisted of continued confusion. She peeked out the window at the even blue cast and couldn't tell what was sky and what was ocean. How can I go in a straight path when I don't know up from down? A thought struck her. She still had the letter to read from her pastor. She reached into the satchel between her legs and pulled out the crinkled note.

> Dear Estaline,
>
> *We have been blessed to have you as an addition at our church. You have been here longer than I have–since the time of your birth. I realize*

it may be heart wrenching to leave familiarity and trod into an unknown. Take comfort that the congregation is praying for you. The transformation you made last year planting the beautiful flowers on our side lot has inspired people's conservation efforts.

The fall is setting in here, but the blooms from the seedlings will continue to inspire. I've been in prayer about you leaving and asked the Lord what advice I may offer you. It is funny because I received several signs and Biblical scripture.

It doesn't make much sense to me, but I'm sure it will to you. He led me to Proverbs 3:5: "Trust in the Lord with all your heart and lean not on your own understanding." Proverbs 3:22–23: "They will be life for you, an ornament to grace your neck. Then you will go on your way in safety."

Thanks be to God,
Pastor Bob

Essa tore at the paper wrapped around the box Vati had given her. It revealed a small, golden, cross-shaped locket. She opened it and inside was a folded message. "When in doubt, pray for guidance." Joy welled in her soul.

Chapter 4

Ryland Baines picked a fragment of lint off his newly bought black interviewing suit and adjusted his lavender tie. He drew in a large breath and exhaled slowly. It was his senior year in business school, and he found himself in a competitive market. The newspaper article he had read said the company sought a temporary researcher who would report to the president of the company. The pay was huge for a first-time job seeker.

He stared at offices of the commercial land development firm in Northern California. The allure of the statuesque, geometric-shaped building whispered intangible promises. Ryland advanced through the main doors and into the lobby. Red paint appeared as though the painter had thrown the can at the wall. Black accentuated the fiery mood.

He stepped up to the desk, and the receptionist glared at him. Her hair was tucked in the back of her head with a tight bun. She wore a plain gray sweater dress, and her face remained stoney. She would be so beautiful if she smiled.

He announced himself, and the woman led him into a

claustrophobic empty room with a computer. She handed him a massive booklet.

"This makes the phone book look like a brochure," he told her, hefting the book. He chuckled nervously.

She stared at him blankly. "You will be taking a personality test and making a statement of your beliefs. When you have completed this, come back to me, and I will send you upstairs to interview with the president." She left, slamming the heavy door behind her.

He shuddered and went through each question, dawdling at first. He sped up as he saw how long it would take him at that pace. He thought it odd that beliefs were needed to land the job. He shrugged it off, and an hour later he had completed it. The woman instructed him to take the elevator up to the thirtieth floor.

Ryland got on and pressed the button. His stomach contracted into a tight ball. He wiped his clammy hands on the hanky that draped from his pocket and attempted to refold it. Soon, the elevator doors slid apart to reveal an open floor plan. Thick, deep red stripes ran along each side of the walls. Blood-red fabric accentuated the diabolical feel. Footsteps echoed down the hall, and a stocky, middle-aged man sauntered toward him in a double-breasted suit coat with suppressed waist. Thick silver rings adorned each finger, and a circle of peppered hair surrounded his head. He made eye contact with Ryland.

A shot went deep into Ryland's soul and intimidated the heck out of him. It must be interview nerves.

"Welcome to my company. You can call me Bockman." The man held out his hand. Ryland nearly didn't shake it for fear of his sweaty palms.

Cold shivers ran up Ryland's arms. A heart-tightening sensation squeezed on his pulse.

"That happens a lot." Bockman's baritone voice vibrated a wicked amusement.

Ryland did not remember showing his fear. *How did he know what I felt?*

He followed the eccentric man down a flight of stairs and through a door. The noise of ringing phones, fingers pounding on keyboards, and conversations overwhelmed him. The employees bustled about, and no one seemed to notice Bockman at all. One would think that as the head of a company, others would be inclined to say hello or nod.

"That will be your office." He pointed to the far right corner.

"I–I'm hired?" Ryland stuttered.

Bockman nodded. "You passed the tests. That is all I needed to know." He motioned for him to follow. He turned to the left, and they passed several offices until they arrived at the last one. "This is my domain," he said.

Ryland looked at how far his office was from Bockman's. As his assistant, he found it peculiar. Maybe it was normal for the real world to be strange.

He opened the door to reveal a deep red office with dark mahogany furniture. An abstract painting of men fighting hung above his black leather chair.

No plants, no pictures, just an immaculate desk and computer. Ryland reminded himself not to run. This was a top-notch opportunity.

Bockman tilted his head and read Ryland's fear. "How is this for a sizeable income?" He turned his computer monitor towards Ryland, angling it with his paltry hands and long, jagged nails.

Ryland's eyes opened even wider. It was far more than he expected.

Bockman nodded at the computer monitor and then looked at Ryland. "That figure will only increase when you do just as I instruct. After a few months, I'll evaluate your performance, and if you're ready, I'll put you on your first project." He got up, walked around the desk, and sat on its side. "You complete the project, and I'll hire you into the firm permanently." His brows rose. "I built this company to go against all others," he continued. "If you want to work here, it will take sacrifice. Understand that you will put your duty to me above all else."

"All—all right."

"Relax." Bockman punched him lightly in the shoulder. "I won't work you to death, but I will work you on Sundays. Those are *mine*, too."

Over the next six months, Ryland learned the business of selling and land development. He had also learned how clandestine Bockman was. There were over twenty people working in the offices on that floor, yet only one person physically saw him at a time. No one knew Bockman's first name, but then, where he came from was just as allusive.

Eventually, Bockman called Ryland to his office. He was holding the file on Hugh Kiebert. Ryland had done impressive research on him, right down to his favorite way to mow his lawn. His field analyst had spent the last week recording Mr. Kiebert's behaviors. Bockman went through with his yellow highlighter and marked points of reference, Keibert's vulnerabilities and predilections. The moment had come to prepare the attack. Bockman sat back in his chair, arms crossed behind his head. "It's project time."

Ryland beamed with pride. He had scoured documents and hacked into computer files. "Hacked" wasn't the right word. What did Bockman call it? An investigation! He told him to think of himself as a detective and to examine tactics to gain the wisdom needed to decide if this man might be a fit for their needs. Ryland had done his job, and now he was going to be trusted with Bockman's high priority case.

"How does Hawaii sound?" Bockman asked.

Chapter 5

Hugh Kiebert had lived his entire life in a metropolis. It provided everything: any kind of food at any time of night, replaceable people to take care of his home, his car, and finances. He didn't even need to ever step foot in a grocery store. There was someone to do that as well. But there was no one to fix his marriage, fourth marriage, to be exact, all packaged with the same issues. Sure, there were people to hear you talk and suggest tools, but no one who could go in and repair it. Lord knew he'd made mistakes, and so had she.

That's why when the call came alerting him to a new opportunity, he took a risk. A better life? Maybe. Same problems? Definitely. He was grasping at straws at this point.

He decided to take the day off, and as CEO of the company, he had the ability. A little guilt set in, but some fast self-talk took care of it. He had put in sixty hours a week, traveled, dwelt with on-call situations each weekend, and prepared for almost anything. He deserved a break.

He pushed together the disarray of papers on his desk, placed the pen back in the caddy, and grabbed his briefcase.

Light between the Leaves

His VP caught him walking out of the office. "Hugh, I'll meet you in the boardroom in five."

"I e-mailed you the presentation. You'll do fine," Hugh reassured him. He continued down the hall to the elevator.

The VP leapt across a line of people coming and going and raced to catch up. "What are you talking about? This is your project lead. I'm only there to nod my head while you describe the trickle down."

"Note cards, my friend, note cards. I sent those to you, as well." Hugh slapped him on the back and kept going.

Hugh recalled a happy tune that was playing on the radio that morning, but he had flipped through the channels and settled on jazz instead. He whistled to the melody of "Singin' in the Rain" and walked out of the building to his car.

This will be a turning point, he decided. I can do it with just about any company. I can do it in marriage. Wait till she gets a sight of this! He laughed and started the engine.

When he pulled into his driveway, he practically leapt from the car and flew into the house with excitement.

"Tasha?" He took a running slide on the heated marble floor of the dining room. No one was home. He rang her cell phone. Her voice message answered. "Dear, call me as soon as you can. No worries." He hung up and finished making arrangements.

He sat on their egg-shell leather couch, put his feet up, and grabbed a recipe magazine from the coffee table. He waited. After forty-five minutes passed with no call from his wife, he rang her again.

"What are you doing calling me during the day? Is everything all right?"

"Yes, I mentioned that on your voice mail. Why didn't you pick up?"

"I'm under the blow dryer right now, my hands and feet, that is. How was I supposed to answer while getting my nails done?" She heaved a lofty sigh.

"I took today off work and for the weekend as well." He paused for effect. "I've got something incredible up my sleeve."

"I have plans." Her coolness struck across his heart. "You can't do whatever you want and expect me to jump."

He felt it was deserved. He had always put her and their marriage last, but he was determined to at least try to make things right this time. He seized the silver picture frame on the table. A random person had taken that of them while they ran along the banks of Quinnipiac River with smiles larger than the bridge in front of them. That was when they were dating. It was their favorite picture, even compared to their traditional wedding shot.

Every thing was the way it should have been. There were disagreements, but they had the time to mend them. They even had the time together to get *involved* in a disagreement. He was offered a promotion and knew it meant more hours. The money and prestige was too much for them not to agree to. It would be easy to blame the time away from her on the profession, but everyone has choices. He chose his career.

"When can you come home?" he asked.

"I promised Nancy I'd pick her up. We're going shopping."

"Could you give me an estimated time?"

"She mentioned dinner at this new bistro she found."

"Tasha, break that and come home. I need to tell you something."

She grumbled and hung up without a word.

Her quick steps on the floor woke him from his nap. He lifted himself off the pillow and checked his watch. It was four o'clock on the nose.

"I'm here. Happy? Now, what is this all about?" She folded her arms.

He walked over to her, uncrossed her arms, and handed her the picture "Remember that couple?"

She didn't know what to say.

"I want that again. We can get back there, and I know how."

He took her hand and pulled her to the closet. "Get your coat on. We have somewhere to be."

Hugh had covered the backseats of their Bentley with hundreds of tiny purple lilac petals. The scent was heavenly. She stared at him in silence.

The chauffer drove them to the airport and parked outside of a private hanger.

"I rented a plane." Hugh explained.

"Where on earth are you taking me?"

"Taking us," he corrected.

Several hours later, they landed and were escorted to a car. It wound them around the countryside of South Africa. They finally reached a circular thatched building with modern décor. Hugh took her by the hand and led her inside to the reception desk, where he signed for the keys to a private bungalow. The back of the lobby opened outside, where they could see a bridge connecting the bungalows.

Tasha ran to the tallest part of the arch and looked out at the short green-covered trees exposed throughout the nature preserve. A large cheetah was stretched out. Its eyes were lined in black, with thin black trails running along its nose, down the dotted cheeks, and into its mouth.

"Look how big its ears are," Tasha said.

Hugh gazed at his wife taking in the new environment. Her guard was down, and he could see her personality come back.

They walked the rest of the way to their private bungalow. The room was open. The last rays of sunlight diffused through the two glass walls showcasing the views. A large taupe-colored tree trunk stood in the corner. The room had been built around it. Mosquito netting hung over the queen-sized bed. Hugh looked for the bathroom.

Tasha walked out the sliding door and onto the balcony. Tiny lanterns on the floor led to an outdoor rock shower and toilet. "I found it!" she called.

Traditional African food was brought to them on the veranda for dinner. The waiter set the plates before them and explained their dishes. *Umphokoqo*, a salad made of maize meal, *vetkoek*, fat cake, deep fried dough balls, and a stew made with a flower of Cape Pondweed. They allowed the night to unfold peacefully, listening to the diverse sounds of nature. They went inside their room. He pulled her close and cradled her in his arms. Their lips met in gentle nudges.

An African love poem had been laid across their bed. It was written in both English and Swahili, side by side. Hugh read the English version.

Light between the Leaves

In Praise Of Love

Give me a writing board of Indian wood,
ink and a precious pen,
let me praise love for you.

It has entered my heart
forsooth, oh pupil of my eye,
you are like cool antimony.

I will care for you, come to me,
like my eldest child,
your love is not half as strong as mine.

Let me praise love for you
let me tell you what I feel,
so that you can look into my heart.

My heart is full of love,
if it had a lid,
I would open it for you.

For you I would open it,
so that you would know my love,
it is bursting my inmost being.

It is splitting my inside,
and yet I feel no pain,
so much do I love you.

Joy is the fruit of love,
when my purpose is accomplished
I will give you a present for life.

I will not leave you all my life,
until death may follow,
may we live in mutual affection.

Nipa loho ya kihindi
wino na kalamu kandi
nikuswifie mapendi.

Yameningia moyoni
kwa sahihi ya aini
kana wanja wa machoni.

'Takutunza uje kwangu
kana wa kwanza mwanangu
yako si nusu wa yangu.

Mapendi nikuswifie
nilo nayo nikwambie
moyoni unangalie.

Umejaa pendo lako
Lau una kifiniko
ningalifunua kwako.

Kwako ningalifunuwa
mahaba ukayajuwa
ya ndani huyapasuwa.

Hunipasuwa ya ndani
wala uchungu sioni
kwa kukupenda fulani.

Sururi tunda ya huba
yatimupo matilaba
heyati takupa hiba.

Sikuachi kwa heyati
hata yafwate mauti
na tuishi kwa widati.

—Author unknown

A man dressed in brown fatigues pointed his binoculars toward the Kiebert's villa. He wore his Bockman Developers baseball cap backwards. The couple was kissing inside the room. He flipped open his cell phone and dialed Bockman. "Time to move on it," he reported.

Hugh's business cell rang on the bedstand.

Tasha groaned.

He kissed her forehead and in a swift motion clutched the phone. The number calling was blocked. He stepped out onto the deck and slid the door closed.

"I have an enticing offer for you." The man on the line sounded sly and confident.

"Who is this, and how did you get my number?" Hugh asked.

"Your profile caught my eye. How would you like to have a career working less hours for more pay and in an exotic locale?"

Hugh tightened his face. "I'm not interested, sorry."

"Your wife?" The man said.

That was the trigger. Hugh remained on the line. "What about her?"

"Wouldn't you want to make this marriage work, avoid another divorce, and be happy for once in your life?"

"How did you kn–."

"I just faxed the job description to the resort's front desk. It has my name, Bockman, on it. It will be waiting for you when you're ready." Bockman hung up.

Hugh stared across the sprawling grounds. Could a career change be the key to a better future? They needed something to force them both out of their rut. He called through the door to his wife. "Sweetheart, I'll be back in ten minutes."

"I don't see the point of getting away if you refuse to leave your work." She wrinkled her face.

"Exactly." He went to get the fax.

He sat outside late at night, inspecting every detail of the CEO position at Planet Care. Being the head of a non-profit would drop his salary, but Bockman was willing to make up the difference for the first year. He decided to accept it without talking to Tasha. He took the reins. Their marriage needed a change, starting now.

Chapter 6

The flight touched down on the tropical tarmac shortly after eleven in the morning that Saturday. Essa could feel the weight of the water vapors in the air. They stepped off the airport gate and made their way toward the baggage claim. Native women and men in grass skirts greeted them, the women wearing bikini tops. They greeted visitors with a thick kaleidoscope of necklaces made from orchid blossoms.

A man dressed in a wild array of colors waved a sign above his straw hat. "ALOHA, Estaline Cassell!"

"Who is that?" Willa asked.

Essa shrugged. "Maybe someone sent from the college to pick us up."

They dragged their luggage over to the man. He smiled excitedly.

"Pastor Bob called me to make sure you had a proper welcome from your new congregation!" He extended his hand. "I'm Pastor Gill. How was your flight?" He took their luggage and put it on a cart he had ready.

"Long!" Willa rubbed her eyes.

"I'm going to get you both over to your apartment so you can rest. Our youth group is having a mountain bike expedition today, but it doesn't start until later this afternoon."

Essa nodded to Willa. "So much for worrying about making new friends."

They stepped into the fresh Hawaiian air. She looked down the city streets. Traffic whisked in and out of lanes, and sky risers dotted the landscape.

Not at all what I was expecting, she thought.

The girls piled into Pastor Gill's navy-blue minivan and sped towards the outskirts of town. He turned left at the sign for the apartment complex. A beautiful fountain shot sprigs of water in the middle of the circular drive.

Essa climbed out of the van. Plant life decorated the spaces with an overwhelming variance of vibrant greens. Bushes with brilliant, yellow bell-shaped flowers lined the building. Their smelled tickled her nose. The white-washed walls reminded her of a mission trip she had taken to Mexico.

The pastor helped the girls find their unit and took their bags inside. "I know you have just arrived, but I really didn't want you to miss the mountain biking. It's a great way to see the island. You'll get exercise from being cramped in the plane and a chance to meet the other members."

Essa's thankfulness was nearly as great as her exhaustion. What a blessing. Any thoughts of loneliness dissipated. She attempted to hide a yawn, but he noticed without commenting.

"I'm going to let you ladies get some rest. I'll have Taylor, our youth leader, come pick you both up at four. After the ride, we'll all grab some dinner. Sound good?"

"Sounds great!" Willa said.

When he was gone, Essa looked around at the vaulted ceilings and spacious floor plan. Beige Berber floored each room, with the exception of the large saltillo tiles in the kitchen and foyer.

"This place comes furnished, too?" Willa walked into the living room, "You didn't mention that, Essa." She sat on the rattan couch.

Essa pointed at the papasan in the corner. "That one is all mine tonight!"

Willa turned her head to the sliding door. "Look!" She got up and motioned for Essa to follow. The glass doors revealed the view of raw Hawaiian nature. The tiny green lawn gave way to eight feet of lush bushes. A foggy mountain looming in the distance provided a backdrop to the yard.

They brewed some lemon tea in the kettle Essa had found on the stove and sipped the soothing drink in the living room, enraptured by the view outside.

Her bedside alarm screeched in pulses. Essa could scarcely remember meandering into the bedroom earlier and laying her head on the fluffy pillow. She smacked the alarm button. She sat up on her elbows and wiped the sleepies from her eyes. Essa unzipped her luggage lying on the bedroom floor and rifled through its contents.

"Throwing clothes around, are we?" Willa said from the doorway to the bedroom.

Essa giggled at Willa's white, knee-high socks. "Nice socks," she said and threw another blouse to the floor. "I'm trying to find something suitable that I can get muddy."

"What about a simple t-shirt and shorts?"

The doorbell rang, and Willa held up her hand. "you finish getting dressed, Miss Essa, and I will get the door."

Essa found a long-sleeved shirt and was able to rip the sleeves off. She slid on her satiny red shorts with slits on the sides—her favorite since she had found them in a thrift shop that dated back to the 80s.

She walked into the living room to find Willa chatting with a gangly girl donning a blonde pony tail. Taylor introduced herself and led them to her white Hyundai Genesis Coup parked in front of the apartment.

They pulled up to a sports shop that looked like a log cabin with a welcoming porch. Pastor Gill stood against the side and checked out a map. A guy with naturally dark skin rolled a Honda CRF dirt bike onto the trailer of a pick-up truck. His dark, short curls were covered in caramel highlights that hinted at many days under the Hawaiian sun.

She got out of the car and shut the door. The guy turned and looked straight into Essa's eyes. He flashed a flirtatious smile. Her breath caught. Essa was so distracted that she lost footing on the gravel. She wobbled forward and steadied herself with her hand on the ground. She pretended to tie her shoe lace and turned away, mortified, hoping he couldn't see the fire burning her cheeks.

Taylor called to her and Willa, "Follow me into the store, and we'll get you helmets and protective gear."

They velcroed knee and elbow pads to their bodies, and each took a backpack already crammed with a first aid kit, water bottles, and snacks.

Essa tried lifting the heavy bag. "What else is in this?"

"Rubber boots and rain poncho, but you can take your shoes off now and put the boots on. We'll be getting dirty." Taylor handed her a bottle of mosquito repellant.

Essa leaned her head close to Willa and whispered. "What did we get ourselves into?"

They joined a bunch of youth gathered outside.

"Listen up!" Pastor Gill said. "It's about a fifteen minute drive to the beginning of the trail. Once we get out there, I will go over how to operate these bikes to any of you who have not had the experience. This four-mile trek will take us through breathtaking terrain, but remember, it rains often, so take care that you don't get stuck in any mud."

He divided them into three groups and handed each person a helmet before climbing into the bed of the truck. They sat on blue and white coolers filled with refreshments. Essa's adrenaline flowed. Now that she was finally here, she was going to get to see the gorgeous nature she had only studied in books.

They came to an expansive field covered with orange dirt. Three trails branched off in different directions. Each person was assigned to a bike and rolled it off the trucks.

"Stay close to me." Taylor squeezed her helmet over her head and flipped the visor. "I've been on these trails before."

"I'll be teaching a botany class at the university," Essa said. "Could you point out some of the vegetation along the way?"

"I know most of the popular trees, but there are so many that I may not remember the names of all of them."

Willa rolled her eyes. "This is supposed to be fun, not a college class," she grumbled to Essa.

The guide explained how to use the bikes, and they lined up on the eastern trail.

Essa jumped on the pedal with force and sped after Taylor, with Willa trailing swiftly behind.

The orange dirt felt well packed below the tires. Shock absorbers sprang her up and down, and the feel of freedom made her smile beneath the heavy helmet. Long grasses lined the path. The sky was mostly clear, with only a few clouds shadowing the miles of island she could see in front of her.

The line of bikers followed a mild slope into a valley of short weeds and wild flowers. Essa caught a whiff of buttercups. The rain forest was just ahead. Tall, tropical trees sheltered the lush ferns below. Branches crackled under the tires. The woods were thick with brush. She crossed a slow-running rocky stream, and cool water splashed her ankles.

Taylor lifted her arm and indicated that they should stop. Essa and Willa pulled up next to her.

Essa lifted her visor. "Is everything all right?" she shouted above the bike engines.

Taylor grinned. "See that tree with the large leaves to your left?

The leaves had marks all over them. She turned off her engine, popped the kick stand, and walked over to it.

"That's an Auto tree. People write their names, message, or even love notes on the leaves. I've even heard stories of them being used as playing cards."

Essa held one and saw a tic-tac-toe game. She giggled, amazed at the plant's durability.

"Anyway, I wanted to show you that. We should probably catch up with the group now." Taylor started her bike again.

They continued up a winding rocky path. She saw a clearing ahead where the others had gathered side-by-side. As she closed in, she could see a cliff overlooking the ocean. Trees grew randomly along the shelf. They resembled pines, but she knew they were Casurinas, a type of ironwood.

Essa pulled up alongside the other bikes. The white-capped waves exploded along the rock wall of the island. A strong wind shifted the pieces of unsecured hair around her baseball cap.

The guy Essa noticed earlier, the handsome one who caused her to stumble, got off his bike and walked over to her. He snuck up behind her.

Taylor saw him and was about to say something. He placed his finger over his lips, motioning for her to be quiet. He leaned towards Essa and whispered, "Look over there." He pointed out to sea.

She jumped at the sound of his voice and turned towards him. His face was inches away. Her eyes couldn't help but notice his full lips. It would be so easy for him to steal a kiss. She whipped her head in the direction he requested.

"I don't see anything," she whispered back.

"You know, your voice is like an angel," he said. He looked at her a little too long for comfort before turning back to the water. He pointed once more.

She squinted and saw the curved dark crest rising from the water.

"That's a humpback whale," he said. "If we're lucky, maybe we'll get to see more."

She stood in silence and watched the whale slip into the depths.

"I haven't seen you before," he said.

"I–I just moved here."

"My name's Ryland, but friends call me Ry." He held out his hand to her.

She placed hers in his. "Essa."

He lifted her hand and kissed the back of it softly. Her pulse quickened. All thoughts escaped her, and she felt lost in the moment. He lowered her hand, smiled, and gave a salute. "See ya' on the trails."

She felt as though he had turned her into a statue.

Pastor Gill's raspy voice broke through the air. "We're at the half-way mark. It looks like you all are holding up well." He walked over to one of the bikers. "Let's all take hands and pray."

They bowed their heads and offered up thanks and praise to God for His glorious creations.

"I've always got to add scripture," Pastor Gill explained. Some of the others chuckled knowingly. "Proverbs 3:18, 'Her ways are pleasant ways, and all her paths are peace. She is a tree of life to those who embrace her; those who lay hold of her will be blessed.' "

The mention of a tree caught Essa's attention. First a seed, now the symbolism of a tree. *God, are you sending me signs?*

They broke up and started their bikes again. Soon they were riding valleys and ancient rock terraces.

Chapter 7

Essa awoke the next morning to find Willa sitting at the dining room table in her thin pink robe, mulling over the phone book.

"Where did you find that?" Essa asked.

Willa looked up from her mug. "It was in the kitchen drawer." She sipped her coffee.

"Isn't it too warm here to drink that?"

Willa laughed. "I'm hooked on the flavor. It's Kona!" She flipped another page and jotted something on a piece of paper. Essa dragged her tired feet over to the table. She sat down and rubbed her eyes. "What are you doing?"

"I'm trying to find you a craft shop. You've gotta have more to do here besides teach class and grade homework."

"I think that will be plenty!"

"Scrapbooking releases tension and lets your creative side flow." She took another sip and circled a listing in the phone book.

"Fine, give me the number."

Willa picked up her cell phone and dialed. She listened

intently to the voice recording on the other end and jotted down the open times on a pad.

Essa checked her watch. "It is 11 o'clock now. I really slept in."

"Your office isn't far from here, but you'd better start getting dressed if we're ever going to get there."

"You've already done so much around my apartment. You only have a few more days here. Let's spend it at the beach."

"I want to see your snazzy digs, and I'm hoping you'll pose for me while I take pictures of you sitting at your desk looking all studious," Willa teased.

Essa had to think whether she had anything in her luggage that was professional enough to wear. Most of her clothes were in boxes somewhere in the mail between her old home and new one.

The musty office looked like it had been unoccupied for decades.

"Willa, can you do me a huge favor?" Essa asked, arranging the next book on the shelf.

"You slave driver!" Willa said, giggling.

"Dean Sterns was supposed to give me the file on the previous course materials. I need to merge them with some ideas I've gotten approval for. Can you ask him for those? His office is just down the hall."

"I remember seeing it when we passed by. It was the only one with a name plate."

"What do you expect? He is the dean."

Willa placed the dusty rag and disinfectant on the floor and stepped into the hall. The hall was quiet except for mumblings behind doors. She found Dean Sterns' door closed. Sounds of a heated discussion echoed from inside. She looked around and pressed her ear to the solid wood door.

"I understand, Bockman, and I intend to retire after this

school year." She only heard two voices, so that one must be the dean, making the other one someone named Bockman.

"You can't ignore the funding issue. People want to financially support new technology, not trees in your backyard," Bockman was saying. "The only way to keep the botany program from going under is to get some incredible research finding."

"We don't have anyone to do that. I just hired Miss Cassell, but it will take her time to get used to things, and she is fairly young."

"No one is going to support that. It has to go. Make this her first and last class she teaches." The dean said something that Willa couldn't catch, but Bockman cut him off. "Sell us the land, and you'll be able to retire without ever having to worry about money again."

"I don't know. Our college has always prided itself as ecologically driven and . . . ."

"Your wife will be happy, and your daughter will be able to get the medical attention she needs for the rest of her life," Bockman said. "I can take care of that. You and the misses will have a house built to your specs free and clear, right on the new resort. You can take advantage of all the amenities at no charge—forever, Mr. Sterns. Why, I'll even give you first pick of the lots. Oceanside, if you wish."

Over the sound of Stern's sigh, Willa heard an echo of footsteps and raced back to Essa's office.

"Did you get them?" Essa inquired.

"Uh, no. He was busy." Willa's heart raced. "I waited though. He just has a lot on his plate right now." She took the spray bottle in hand and began cleaning.

"You already cleaned the desk." Essa arched one brow and continued filing.

Willa lifted their water bottles and shook them. "I'll go refill these." She needed an excuse to get out of there before she said something she shouldn't.

She walked down the hall opposite of the dean's office and

found the stairwell. How am I going to explain to Essa that her program is going to be nonexistent? Willa tipped the bottles under the faucet. She thought that telling Essa she had to look forward to going back would be a slap in the face. It would be better if she heard it from the dean and not from me. It's not like it's official yet. I could be starting a nasty rumor if I said anything. It would get around the school, and the professors might start jumping ship. Then they really wouldn't have a program anymore! Even if Dean Stern's decides to drop the major, that would take time, and Essa could have years under her belt before having to find another job. No, I can't tell her.

Willa returned to the office to find Essa looking out the window. "Never forget you can make a huge impact," Willa told her.

Essa turned her head. "I can't believe I'm hearing this from you."

"Hearing what?" Willa's eyes widened, and she wondered if her friend could read her mind.

"A positive comment on me relocating here. I think you finally understand why I wanted to come."

"I'm willing to bet that it will offer quite the challenge, but it's one I know you can handle."

Saying goodbye to Willa proved difficult. After spending the week together, the feeling of loss hit the inner-most chamber of Essa's heart. She didn't know when she would see her best friend again. Essa took the pillow from the couch Willa had been sleeping on to put it away. Underneath, she found a small rectangular box. She lifted the top to reveal a stainless steel watch. Its face was in the shape of a triangle. The thick band looked like a bangle bracelet. A note was taped underneath it in Willa's hand writing: "So you will never be late to change to world."

Her soul filled with gratitude as the weeks followed. She had new friends to rely on. Amana, her teaching assistant, helped her get acquainted with the new culture, trying different foods and understanding the passion the Hawaiians had for their land. She was invited to weekend luncheons at the house of Amana's grandma, Meli.

Taylor surprised her one day by showing up at her apartment with an auto tree. "Everyone who comes to visit you can carve their name in it," she said. Essa placed the heavy pot near the sliding glass doors to give the plant lots of sunshine.

She was comfortable with Pastor Gill's church and attended each Sunday and Wednesday nights for Bible study and dinner. Ryland usually sat next to her, and they worshiped together. She warned him about her inability to carry a tune and wondered how he could stand to listen to it. He explained that she carried happiness in her voice and that it helped mask any wrong notes.

She had grown accustomed to teaching and enjoyed her routine. She knew this was not only where she wanted to be but also the place where she needed to be.

Chapter 8

Essa chained her bike to the water-beaded rack outside the parking garage and bolted across the sheets of rain to her classroom. This was the last session to teach for the semester, and she was looking forward to the break. The room was brimming with noisy chatter. The densely packed students made it hot and stuffy. She laid her umbrella down and threw her rain jacket over the projector cart. She glanced at her wrist and realized she was only five minutes late. She took a step up to the podium and caught her breath.

"Look upward with your mind's eye," she began. She commanded attention with a pause. "Picture an immense, upside-down tree reaching its many strong branches toward you to grasp. You cannot touch it without raising your hand. The deep greens of the leaves drip a tepid, watery mist to the tips of your fingers. What you are seeing is real." Her passion reached each soul in an earthly reality. She could see them react to the image. "Scented flowers of yellow and its softened, rain-soaked fruit suspend among the protective boughs." She inhaled deeply. "The leafy flesh gradually warms in the encompassing light, carrying nourishment through its veins."

Light between the Leaves

The room was silent except for the hum of computers. Essa strode across the platform she called her safe zone. There, Essa allowed herself the confidence to speak freely without fearing judgment. Her spirit of faith did not waiver. As she scanned the room, she could tell her attempt at representing heaven colliding with earth was taking hold.

"The Tree of Life is fogged in mystery and suffers great debate. In this class, we dare to examine its reason for being here and its historical significance to diverse groups around the world." Essa tipped the laser pointer in her hand to the screen depicting the acacia tree. "Does anyone recognize this species?"

A native girl raised her hand. Essa nodded to her. "It's found on Maui and is the Acacia Confusa." She squinted her eyes from the light reflecting on the screen. "It was planted there to act as a windbreaker."

"Correct. It is *not* native to Hawaii, yet it adapted. What meaning does this tree hold and by whom?" Her question alluded to the theme of today's lesson. A few pupils leaned forward with interest. It was easy for Essa to determine the botany majors from the others. Some minds interpreted it as an unimportant elective course, just one among many that would make up a long, forgotten moment of their journey.

A deep voice answered from the back corner of the dark room. "Thanks to a religious history class, I think I can take a stab at this one." Essa recognized Ryland's voice and waited for him to continue. Ryland Baines was not a botany major but a pre-med student. Just last week, he had fallen asleep in her class, only to awake with a shout from a dream. He straightened his orange polo shirt and leaned back in the creaky wooden seat. "There are three main perspectives." He counted on each finger. "The Jewish, Freemasonry, and Christian view. The Jewish tradition contains a pictorial representation of the Etz Chaim—the Tree of Life."

Amana stood at a computer to the left of the stage. She rummaged through the slides on her laptop. "We have this," she whispered to Essa. The image popped onto the screen behind them. She pointed at herself and then to the center of the room, eyebrows arched in a silent question. Essa nodded.

Amana stepped up to the platform. "As Ryland stated, this pictorial image is known as the Sephirot. It is a conceptual model revealing God's will. There are ten circles of characteristics. The top is labeled as the Divine, and middle circle is listed as the Tree of Life." She began twisting the large, V-shaped beads on her bracelet.

Essa glanced at Amana's nervous habit and came to her rescue. Amana didn't care for speaking before large groups. She was better suited for leading afternoon tours at Planet Care. "The Sephirot outlines God's plan as it unfolds itself into creation. The ten circles were derived from the ten utterances God spoke to create the world referenced in Genesis in the Bible. We won't go into more detail in this as we're focusing on botany."

Amana took a deep breath and gathered her thoughts. "The freemasons view the Tree of Life as resurrection and immortality. This is widely accepted with several cultures. They also see this as an example for the soul's persistence through life."

"I concure," Essa broke in. "Amana, would you offer up the Christian significance?"

"Eastern Christianity recognizes the Tree of Life from various parts of the Bible. They consider the acacia the Tree of Life." She spoke in a quickened pace and explained how each part of the plant held specific meaning. "The weeds and thorns that attempt to choke the tree are represented as the sins of humanity. The seed is God's word; the root system symbolizes Jesus. The tree, like the freemasons believe, is symbolic of immortality. Its leaves are considered to bring healing, and the flowers stand for the glory of God. The fruit is His unfailing love for humanity."

Essa nodded her approval of Amana's explanation. "No one is sure if this one tree exists anymore. If so, it is said in the Bible that angels with swords of fire are protecting it within the garden so no one can enter."

Light between the Leaves

"Why did God use a tree to describe this?" the native Hawaiian asked.

Amana explained, "We are not the same entity as God; therefore, matter of some sort exists between us. Humans do not possess the intelligence level of God. One method of communication He utilizes with humans is signs and images."

She took a step down and walked to the side of the classroom. "In Karl Rahner's view, if God wants to reveal himself to human beings, then He must enable human beings to receive Him through material objects we understand. Therefore, God must reveal himself through material objects so that human beings can overcome the limits of the world and meet God as transcended beings."

Essa called out, "Time is up. See you all at the final exam."

Amana began putting away the electrical equipment. Essa reorganized her papers and filed them in her satchel. She gave Amana a wave. "See you next week." She headed to the door outside. She saw Ryland walking ahead of her. "Wait up!"

He turned around and locked a tight gaze on her face. She fumbled to gain control of the books in her arm. One fell to the cobblestone walkway with a loud thud. He walked around a bed of purple lilies and leaned down to pick it up. He read the title aloud, "Hawaii's Botanical Resources. Looks great."

"You know, I had no idea you were a student in my class until I received the roster a day before the semester started."

"Why do you think I took it?"

She tilted her head in a thoughtful way. "Would you have time to grab some coffee? I'm curious to hear why you decided to learn about botany when you are clearly intent on pre-med studies."

"I do have time and can explain." Of course, he wasn't going to tell her that Bockman had suggested he take a class in that department to get information from the inside. He hadn't realized that it was the class Essa was teaching. The pre-med major acted as a front. He had his business degree and planned to stay in property development. He chewed on his fingernail and wondered how long he would be able to continue the charade.

They walked toward the coffee shop.

"Ever considered switching majors?"

"No. I took this class as an elective to learn more about the *healing* properties of plants." He wiped the beads of sweat beginning to form on his forehead. He hated having to lie. Not that it mattered.

They stopped in front of the restaurant, and Ryland held the door for her to enter. They ordered their tailored beverages and found the last table available, right next to the noisy grinding of the coffee machines and froth makers. Essa inhaled the mix of aromas.

"You're quite the nerd, you know," Ryland said. "What drove you to plants?"

She scoffed, placed her hands around the warm mug in front of her, and scrunched her shoulders. "I grew up in a rural community. One day, I dared to think of how God made things and why." She took a sip of her chocolate mocha. "Much later, God showed me how to hear His answers to my questions in scripture. It brought about the understanding that there's not a transfer of His abilities *into* signs, but through them He stretches out His hand to us like a branch of an upside down tree. Hence, my lecture this morning. We meet by reaching toward Him. Otherwise, we cannot ascend *to* Him. I trust He wants people to remember that their lives spring from Him, so He gives them symbols and evidence, such as trees, of His love for us."

Ryland gazed at her. "If He didn't love us so much, He wouldn't have bothered with nature's beauty and our enjoyment."

A hue of pink blanketed her cheeks. Ryland realized that his last comment could have been taken more than one way. He took a swallow of his drink.

Essa looked away a moment and then nodded towards a man

with a black fedora. "Wasn't that guy sitting next to you in class?" she asked him.

"I don't remember," he lied. Ryland took a deep breath. "I also have another reason for taking this class." He lifted his eyes from his coffee. "You may think this is crazy."

Essa giggled. "How bad could it be? I'm nutty about plants. The pun was intended."

Pun? Whatever. He peered around the room. "That tree you've been talking about–the Tree of Life." He leaned against the table and lowered his voice. "I've seen it."

She stared at him through narrowed eyes.

"I've had dreams and visions, if you will. That's why I've had trouble getting a good night's rest and sometimes fall asleep in class."

"It's not because my lectures are boring? That's a relief." She leaned on her elbows and rested her chin in her hand. "Go on then. Tell me about these dreams."

"I am scuba diving in the ocean . . . playing with the fishes, you know, milling about. Then I come across this gianormous tree, fully leafed."

"And this is underwater in the ocean?"

"Yes."

"I've known several plants that live submersed and look as though they are on land. There is even a hobby for aquarists who make mini underwater 'worlds' in their fish tanks. Some look like the desert, some a deciduous forest. It's pretty cool."

"But not the Tree of Life."

She regarded him quizzically. "I–I guess I'm not understanding."

"Let me approach this a different way. Have you ever received signs you've believed from God?"

"Yes, I mean, I think so. It's common for believers to safely assume a sign is from God if it happens three or more times and the Holy Spirit reveals it is from Him. Albeit, He seems to stay hidden in the background of our lives, creating a need for faith."

Ryland nodded.

"What are you getting at?" Essa questioned.

"I think what I saw is real and here in Hawaii. I want to investigate it. I feel like God is leading me."

"How on earth would you find the image from your visions out there in the vastness of the ocean?" she asked.

"I called my pastor back home in California to help me interpret this. I asked him how I would know if God is speaking to me."

"I thought you told me you were from Africa."

"My parents are, but I was born in the States."

"What did he say?" She knitted her slender brows.

"He told me to look up a few verses in the Bible and pray about it." He unzipped his gray back pack and pulled out a worn leather Bible.

"It is well documented throughout the Bible that God shows signs, wonders, miracles, and gifts of the Holy Spirit. Look." He pointed at the scriptures. "It's warned that we should be careful, as it reads in Second Thessalonians 2:9, 'The coming of the lawless one will be in accordance with how Satan works. He will use all sorts of displays of power through signs and wonders that serve the lie.' " He flipped to Acts 2:22 and began to read. " 'Jesus of Nazareth was a man accredited by God to you by miracles, wonders and signs, which God did among you through him, as you yourselves know.' "

Essa thought for a moment, then said, "That seems to tell me to pray after you believe you've received a sign to ensure it is from Him."

"Yes," he agreed, "and listen to the Holy Spirit, which He speaks through. I've had many a time when my soul has felt uneasy and confused, then also times when it has felt a calmness and peace. The former being of God.

"I can say I'm Christian," Essa told him, "but I have got to confess that I'm working on my personal relationship with Him." She lowered her head. "I've allotted most of my time to work, and I need a better balance in my life."

"Keep coming to our youth group at church."

She nodded her head, first slightly, and then in a more pronounced agreement. "When are you going to tell me about these dreams? Did God show you it was from Him?"

"I believe so, yet I'm not sure how He wants to use me or to what extent." He went on to explain, "When I fell asleep last night, the same visions came. I was scuba diving and went through several obstacles to get to the tree."

"What were they? Did you have any idea where?"

"It wasn't revealed what the obstacles were, but there was a boat that I surfaced to. As I was coming up to the air from my decompression, I saw the letters on the back of the craft. It was so clear."

"Let me guess." She rolled her eyes upward, and then back to him. "The boat was named Heaven."

He chuckled. "That would be too much! No, the letters were NW and the word 'Pearl.'"

"My teaching assistant, Amana, is a native from Hawaii. I bet she might have some insight on this." Essa sipped the final drop from her mug. "She works as an ecological guide."

Ryland popped up from his chair and pushed it in.

"What are you doing?" Essa asked. "Leaving so soon?"

"Let's go."

"Where?"

"Is Amana there right now?"

The man with the black fedora pretended to read his newspaper in the coffee shop. He took his cell phone out of his pants pocket.

"Sterns, this is Bockman. My plan will be intensified. There is more to this web than I expected, but I'm going to make it work for our benefit. Meet me in your office in fifteen minutes."

It may have been Stern's office, but Bockman made himself at home. He rested one leg on Stern's desk and dialed the phone. He pushed the conference button and hung up the receiver.

"What is this about?" Sterns asked, annoyed at Bockman's behavior.

Bockman raised a finger to shush him.

The phone rang once before the recipient picked up.

"This is Hugh Kiebert."

Bockman grinned and asked, "How are you liking Hawaii so far?"

Sterns raised a brow in confusion.

A laugh resonated through the phone's speaker. "Great! Hawaii is a nice change of pace from New York City. I'm getting a guided tour of my new location as we speak."

That would be Amana, Bockman figured. Maybe he should find a use for her, too. "We can expect you tomorrow afternoon. We'll send a limo to your house and bring you to my make-shift office."

"I can't wait," Kiebert replied.

Bockman hung up. "I suppose you'd like to know how I have my pawns set."

"I'm still very confused." Sterns admitted.

Bockman walked over to a chalkboard on the wall. He drew white arrows on the green backing. His pressure on the chalk created a shrill sound. "I've been researching who the best acquisitionist is in the United States."

He paused for effect. "It took me six months to find Hugh. He has an amazing way of acquiring private investors. They are lined up in a row waiting for the final word. Once they hear the deed to the university land is signed over to my firm, I will begin the construction process."

He put his arm around Stern's shoulder. "You get to design your future home. I've got several locals waiting to hear when they can begin work. This partnership we have is bringing jobs and money to the people. I want everything to be smooth, quick, and according to plan."

"I don't recall any university land being up for sale."

"It will be." He thrust a thick stapled document across the desk.

"Even if I would sell you the land, we're in a partnership with Planet Care, and they are also on the deed. They would have to agree to it as well before it would be sellable."

"That little phone call I just made was to the new CEO of Planet Care. Hugh Kiebert was hired by the Board of Directors for his conservationist attitudes and by me for his signatures." He tilted his head back and laughed. "Of course, they don't know I was the one who sought him and paid him to take this position. Hugh gets a cut of the resort profits. Everyone wins!" He nearly laughed again, but cut himself off, suddenly becoming serious. He leaned across the desk. "Are you in or do we have to make this ugly?"

Sterns let out a sigh.

"The only thing that can get in our way now is that botany teacher you hired last fall. She seems quite passionate about the program. I've got one of my youngest employees acting as a student to ensure we keep on track. Time is money, after all."

"Miss Cassell?"

"That would be the one." The deep wrinkles around his mouth widened. He leaned back and crossed his arms over his head. He had everything set up. It was only a matter of time before he got what he wanted. "My claws are in deep."

Chapter 9

"You want me to get on that thing?" Essa pointed to Ryland's moped parked parallel on the campus lot. She couldn't quite tell whether the moped was supposed to be silver and red or it was just old and worn. A breeze lifted a fleck of red paint, and she watched it float to the pavement.

"Why? Do you have a taxi waiting?" He flashed her a broad smile, and she felt her face grow hot. Well, it was probably safe. She cringed and threw her leg over the ripped seat.

He shoved his thick curls into a Darth Vader-like helmet and handed her a neon yellow one that she guessed was circa 1990.

"So where is this place?" he shouted and pulled out from the stall.

"Take a left on Maile Way out to University Ave," she shouted back above the sputtering motor. She pointed out turns, enjoying the cool wind in her face.

They curved around mountainous terrain and finally pulled into a long drive on a cloud of dust. He parked the bike on the side of Planet Care's offices, a modest, one-story building. She lifted the heavy helmet and felt the squeeze of it against her cheeks and head. A gust whipped off the waves and swirled up the face of the rock walls, causing her hair to billow around her face.

Amana walked out the front door with a tall, thin man dressed in a navy suit. She caught sight of the two and waved. "What are you doing here? I thought you had papers to grade the rest of the morning." She smirked like a mother catching her child in a lie.

"I planned on doing that. It doesn't always go the way you think."

"They do in my case," Amana said.

The man beside Amana reached to shake her hand. "I'm Hugh, the new CEO of Planet Care." His strawberry blonde hair gave color to his clammy skin tone. He turned to Amana. "There will be a lot of changes around here, but only for the better, of course." He chuckled, excitedly.

Amana recognized Ryland from their class. "Essa, may I speak with you for a moment?"

Ryland arched one brow and whispered to Essa. "Is she your keeper?"

"We help each other."

Amana led Essa over to the side of the building, out of hearing range.

"What are you doing?" she asked Essa. "Please tell me you're not getting involved with him." Amana's voice shot up an octave.

Essa realized how her friend viewed the situation. "This is a little strange, I admit." She tried to brush her hair back into place. "He asked me a question only you can answer."

"I don't have time to give him a tour right now."

"This isn't an extra credit assignment for him." She wondered how to approach the question without sounding crazy. "I tried to explain to him he could ask you tomorrow, but he insisted we come see you now. I really didn't see the harm of investigating his inquiry."

"I don't have much time. I've got to drive to the other side of the island and meet a group by noon."

Essa gave her a summary of his dreams and asked if she knew of a boat with the words "NW" or "Pearl."

"Do you realize how many boats there are on Oahu, Essa? There are new vessels coming over from different islands every day." She shook her head. "I may know a few of the ones who have rented the same slip for years, nothing with 'NW.' The word 'Pearl' isn't exactly unique for a boat, you know."

Essa sighed. "Just thought I'd check with you before I sent Ryland on a wild goose chase."

"You have things to get done today and do not have time to indulge in his fantasies."

Essa agreed but thought how exciting it would be to travel around with Ryland, even if they didn't find anything. She wanted a little adventure in her life. Something she wouldn't normally do. She said goodbye to Amana and returned to Ryland.

"Nothing," she said. "Looks like you'll have to do things the time-consuming way and check out the docks yourself."

"How many are there exactly?" he asked. He looked worried.

"At least a dozen. Ships come in and out. Even if there was one with that name, it may be out to sea when you go looking for it."

"What about a list of everyone who rents the slips? There has to be one."

"That would make it a lot easier," Essa agreed.

"Ok, we might as well get started. Show me where to go."

"Ryland, I realize you may have something here, but isn't it kind of farfetched?"

"If you thought God may be speaking to you, would you ignore Him?"

"No," she said with a sigh. "Most of us would love to hear from Him."

"It's faith we go on, Essa."

"I suppose you're right. Let me know what you find." She put her helmet on. "Drop me off at the college in front of the language building."

He turned his head around to face hers. "You're coming with me."

"No, no. I have other things to do today."

"And you have the whole day to do it. But right now you can come with me." He threw her over his rounded shoulders and plopped her on the bike.

"Seriously, Ryland!"

"I'm declining your request." His eyes sparkled in the bright sun. He sent sparks through her skin.

No one told her what to do other than her parents, and that was when she was younger. She didn't know how to respond to his persistence. It was true. She had plenty of time to finish grading papers, but Ryland was her student. There was no way she was going to get involved with him unless it had to do with botany, so there were no worries. Still, it did sound like fun, and, of course, it didn't hurt that he was so handsome.

"Fine," she conceded and gave him directions to the Kewalo Basin harbor.

They came to a stop at the lot adjacent to the boat house and gas station. They got off his bike and walked the concrete catwalk constructed along the boulevard and seaward face of the bay. The fresh aroma of fish flavored the air.

"What are you going to do when or if you find this boat?" Essa asked. A myriad of catamarans, sail boats, and motor boats offered anything from sport fishing to whale watching.

"See where they regularly go and pray about it. God will guide me."

She admired his faithful spirit. He turned onto a dock. A two-level watercraft boasted dive and snorkel charters in large blue letters. Scuba tanks lined the bottom level.

"As I see it, you have conveniently involved me as well, so you had better start praying."

He stopped and looked at her. "I didn't realize you were willing to go the distance with me."

Essa frowned. "The distance? What do you mean by that?"

"We may have to endure crazy stuff to discover what we're looking for."

Essa forced a laugh. As if she weren't doing that already. "Like stifling hot treks through a bug-infested jungle?" Why am I here? she asked herself. He is literally chasing a dream. This has nothing to do with me. "Forgive me, Ryland, but I really need to be getting back." She started to walk away and stumbled.

Ryland reached out to catch her. He laid his arm under her ribs and cushioned her fall. They fell to the pavement, and the weight of her body landed on his forearm. He winced.

Her cheeks turned fuchsia. She shook it off, and he helped her to her feet. "Are you ok?"

He grabbed his arm and rubbed it hard.

"I'm sorry. Are you hurt?" Essa leaned in. Several long red scrapes on his arm started to bleed. Bits of small stone had imbedded into his skin. She used the tip of her fingers to brush them out.

"I'll be all right. I'm tough as nails. It would take a lot more than that to lay me up."

She glanced below at what she had tripped on. Then she saw it, a literal sign. She bent down to pick up a large, tear-shaped seed and looked questioningly at Ryland.

"Who left that here?" He asked and looked around. "This place is immaculate, all except for a seed."

Essa thought she'd give Ryland's scavenger hunt a little more time, on the off chance there was something more to it. "It would be easier to ask the harbor's manager for a list of the boat names. It's public information."

"Great idea."

They walked to the boathouse, and he opened the door for her. A stout man in his forties sat at a simple wood desk and spoke with one of the maintenance staff. "Harvey, it'll take days to order that part and get it shipped here." He straightened his button down shirt when he saw them. "Harvey, we'll talk later. What can I do for you two?"

"We were wondering if you had a list of the boats moored."

"Looking for one specific?" He reclined back in his swivel chair.

"NW Pearl."

"Doesn't ring a bell. Let me check." He typed one finger at a time on the filthy, plastic-covered keyboard.

"Nope," he said.

"Well, thanks anyhow," Ryland replied, and they turned to walk toward the door.

"But I can tell you what the NW means," the man called to them.

Ryland pivoted 180 degrees on the ball of his shoes. "You can?"

"Sure. It refers to the Hawaiian islands northwest of here, or otherwise known as the Marine National Monument. President Bush named it that back in 2006, and it's a United Nations world heritage site." The manager pointed to the map on the wall behind his desk. "If there is one specific boat you are looking for, there are still eight more harbors on the island."

They spanned two other harbors and took a break on a scuffed-up bench overlooking a bay of boats. The waning sun made Essa squint. She looked off to her right, reading the names on the back of the yachts and wondered how they got them. Out of the corner she saw the capital letters 'NW.' She gasped and took Ryland's hand, pulling him toward the pier.

He put one foot in front of the other reluctantly. "Please, no more."

As they got closer, she could see a figure on the sixty-five foot, twin-engine water craft moving against an image of a setting sun. She squinted along the side of the boat to read its full name. "I cannot believe your dream was actually real." She stood with her mouth wide open.

"Wh–what?" He had to read it again to justify what he was seeing.

Essa rang the metal bell off the back of the lower cabin.

An older gentleman turned around and tilted his head. "We're done for the day, ma'am." His face was covered in gray stubble and his hands were filthy from cleaning fish.

"I'm inquiring about the name of your vessel," Essa said in a small voice.

"We take this here craft out to the northwest islands. They only allow those with permits out that way."

"You can't take us out there, can you?"

"It's a three-day journey. Several of the islands 'er tiny with sheer cliffs. Rugged terrain. You studyin' somethin'?"

Essa and Ryland looked at each other.

"Yes," she said. "I'm a botany professor at the university."

"Well, someone at the college should be able to get a permit for ya'. We usually anchor and dingy in, depending on what island yer goin' to."

It dawned on Essa that she wasn't sure where God was leading them. Usually, after the fact, she could look back at what she had gone through to see how events tied together. Looking ahead was not her strength.

"Where would we get an application?"

"I'd think the head of yer department." He placed a hand on his head to shield the bright rays. "I jus' work this boat. Here's a card. Ya' can call the shop where the owner is and ask 'im any other questions."

"Thank you." Ryland took the card.

They walked back to Ryland's moped.

Essa turned to Ryland. "Why do you suppose they won't let other people out there?"

"I don't know, but we'll find out." He started the engine. "Let's ask Dean Sterns."

"I could go after my morning class. How do you know him?"

Ryland paused. "I don't. I mean, when I transferred out here from my other college, he reviewed my classes to see which I could skip on and which I'd have to take."

She wasn't certain why, but her reluctance to trust Ryland returned.

Chapter 10

That night in her apartment, Essa sat cradled in her papasan. She twirled the phone cord around her fingers and could not shake her hesitation to speak with the dean. She leaned down, pulled the boat owner's card out of her purse, and glanced at the clock. She doubted anyone would answer at night. She dialed the number. It rang twice, and someone picked up.

"I was calling in regards to your charter. We would like to visit the northwest islands."

"Are you a scientist?" the man asked.

"I'm a professor at the college and studying the plant life out there."

"Under or above the water? Do you have a captain, or do you need one?"

She had no idea what she needed. Then she remembered Amana drove some of the watercrafts for the eco-tours, but would she know how to drive the charter's boat? "How much would it be for a week with our own driver?"

"The college has an account here. I can bill them separately since we give them a substantial discount."

"We'll need four scuba tanks, as well."

"We can do that. Do you know which atolls you want to look at?"

"Not exactly."

"If it's flora and fauna you're after, then Pearl and Hermes Reef has several herbal plant species. Midway Atoll is about four thousand miles from Honolulu and the only area in the northwest chain where recreational divers can go, but there you would have eighteen locations to dive." He paused a moment. "We're chartering some conservationists tomorrow and will be arriving in three days. If you want to take a flight out to Sand Island of Midway, our boat can meet you."

"It takes three days to get out there?" She slumped in the chair.

"Think of the distance from New York City to Omaha, Nebraska. That is roughly the expanse of the north west archipelago."

The vastness astounded her. "Please book that for us." She tried to sound more confident than she felt. She hoped she could convince Amana and Ryland to go along with this plan.

"Do you have your permit?"

"No. How do I get one?"

"The college has applications in the human resource office. I'm sure it won't take long to get approved."

She thanked the man and hung up. She was about to call Amana when her phone rang. It was Willa.

Willa sounded shaken. "I can't hide this secret anymore."

"What a surprise to hear your voice! What secret?"

"I've been up half the night for a week worried about you! Is everything still all right?"

"Everything's fine. Shouldn't it be?" *What is going on?*

"Remember when I was helping you set up your office?"

"I'm so thankful for that. I miss you! Is this call to tell me you are coming back to visit me?"

"Oh, I wish!" Her concern echoed through the lines.

"I should've told you this awhile ago when I overhead the conversation, but you were just starting this position, and I didn't want to assume anything."

"Willa, what are you talking about?"

"Remember when you had me ask the dean about your files?"

"Please, don't worry about that. I got those files from him."

"That is not what this is about. I overheard Sterns talking with someone else in his office." She hesitated. "The other man was planning to eliminate the botany program."

"I'm sure that was just talk." Essa brushed it off.

"No, the dean admitted to him that you will need major research findings to keep the program's funds. If not, then Sterns and this other guy intend to use the university land designated for the botany program for a resort."

Essa laughed. "The university wouldn't give that away. Besides, I've heard nothing on that, and I continue to get a paycheck."

"You just finished a semester. Do you know if you're going to be teaching the next one?"

"I've been so busy grading finals, which I just turned in, that I haven't touched base with him yet." Essa's heart began to quicken. A whole series of what-ifs ran through her head.

"You know, if it doesn't work out, I would be happy to have you come back home, but I know you want to teach."

"I'm working on research now."

"Then I'm sure the dean will extend the program, knowing that."

"He doesn't know what I'm conducting," Essa admitted.

"Why not?"

"I'll feel silly if what I'm chasing after turns out to be nothing."

"How can you think that? I thought God was directing you. Granted, I don't know what you are up to."

"He is. I just don't know what He is trying to show me. I do know where though. I just chartered a boat out to the northwest islands, hoping that Amana and Ryland will agree to help me. I

Light between the Leaves

can't do it alone. Maybe what I find will be just the thing needed to save the program."

"Essa, what are you searching for?"

"Don't think I'm crazy," she pleaded. It did sound crazy, of course.

"I'm your best friend, and this is coming from God. Who am I to know His plan for you? I am here to encourage you, Essa."

"The Tree of Life."

"The what?"

"Be patient, Willa. I'll explain everything later."

She hung up with Willa and walked into her bedroom. She pulled her blankets back from the pillow and smoothed out the wrinkles. The room suddenly flashed in light. She glanced at the window. A brighter flash shot through the dark sky. If there was one thing she loved besides teaching, it was the fresh smell of rain and seeing what appeared for a second when lightening lit the world. She grabbed her flip flops, scurried out the door, and ran down to the beach.

She was alone. The cool moist sand molded around her feet. She walked along the ocean's edge in the night. Her eyes had adjusted to the dark by the time she got there. The wind quickened its pace and came in gusts, tossing her locks about her face. She tucked the strands behind her ears. The sky lit for a brief moment. The light showed scattered shiny stones. Tufts of deep green sea grasses rustled in the winds. She saw a tall, shadowy figure walking casually in her direction. The person's face was concentrated on the waves. She squinted and recognized him. Ryland. She waved her hands high above her head. It caught Ryland's attention. He stopped, noticed it was her, and started a brisk run.

Her smile widened. "How did you know I was out here?"

"I didn't." He caught his breath. "The sound of the thunder drew me out."

"You've been following me this whole time!" She punched him on the arm, but smiled to show she was teasing.

He chuckled nervously. "The semester is over." He leaned in closer catching a whiff of her soapy smell.

She turned her head. "You're going back to California for medical school, right?"

He lowered his head and kicked the sand around with his feet. "I've been meaning to talk to you about that."

A crack of fork lightening hit the water a hundred yards from them. He placed his arms around her as if to shelter her. It shook the ground under them.

"Let's go inside," he yelled over the thunder.

"Yes, I need to go." She looked directly into his eyes and scrunched her nose. "Alone."

She wasn't sure what spooked her. Maybe it was his directness or the static environment, but tiny shocks swept up and down her arms and legs. She walked faster toward the back of the apartment complex. She unlocked the door to the patio and looked back. Ryland was standing in the same spot, watching her. She turned the handle and went inside.

Chapter 11

The next morning, Essa woke when the light of day had yet to come. She dialed Amana.

"What are you doing, calling me now?" Amana's voice slurred.

"We need to meet. There is so much to figure out."

"Can't it wait until," she paused a moment, "seven or eight o'clock?"

"No, head over to Planet Care and put on a pot of coffee. I'll be there in a few minutes."

She heard a mumble from Amana, and she hung up.

Essa hopped on her ten-speed and made her way toward the winding road up the side of a volcano where Planet Care was situated. The sun was just beginning to rise off the waters when she arrived. One window had a light on. She knocked on it and waved at her friend.

Amana unlocked the door and yawned. Her dark tresses were frizzed and one side stuck up.

"We have so much to figure out. That is why I called Ryland on the way over." She wiggled out of the shoulder straps on her backpack. "He needs to help us pour through this information. I hope we can make sense of it."

"What are you talking about?" Amana lifted a coffee cup to her lips.

"God's messages."

"The Lord did not create me to be a morning person, and He knows I cannot interpret things till afternoon."

Essa gave a fake laugh. "Haven't you ever been in the middle of something, let's say sleep in your case, when an epiphany hits you like a bolt?"

Ryland knocked on the door and came in. "I came as quickly as I could. Is everything all right?"

Essa pulled him in. "To the meeting room." She hurried them toward the chairs. Two rectangular tables were set up along the walls opposite each other. A rear projector was mounted in the back, and a few easels with rolls of white paper stood in front.

"Everybody sit," Essa said.

Amana glanced at Ryland with a less-than-amused expression.

"I spoke with the owner who charters the North West Pearl. He is taking a team of researchers to the islands this morning. It will take him about three days to get out to Midway Atoll where they have a runway and will meet us getting off the plane."

Amana rested her chin in her hand. "If I remember correctly, my grandpa was stationed at Midway in the 1940s. He was a naval officer. I could call my Grandma Meli and ask her about it."

Essa paced with her mug in hand. "That's a good idea. But first, we need to figure out where we are being led, and, most importantly, why." She set her drink on the table and took a blue marker from the tray. "Let's make a list of clues given to us and see what we come up with."

Ryland spoke first. "There are my recurrent dreams about the boat, which turned out to be correct."

"God keeps speaking to me of a seed and Tree of Life," Essa added. "I've asked Him several times to show me my purpose in life, and He keeps directing me. I'm finally taking heed of His signs and listening. That's why I came to Hawaii."

Amana took a small Bible out of her purse. "I think we need to take a few things into consideration. It doesn't hurt to investigate the evidence with gentle guiding from the Lord. What we do need to ensure are any signs of falsity, like is mentioned in Isaiah 44:25, and listen to God, not people. He should confirm our decisions in prayer. Our direction shouldn't be twisted toward self interest but focused on the good and the signs leading us closer to Christ."

Ryland added. "Here is one I have repeated many times. Hebrews 2:4 says, 'God also testified to it by signs, wonders and various miracles, and gifts of the Holy Spirit distributed according to his will.' "

Essa extended her hands toward them. "Let's pray." They took hand and bowed their heads. "Dear Father, help us to be like You, provide us with understanding for Your will and lead us safely. Amen."

Amana smiled. "Let's say we find it. What do we do then?"

"Back up. We still need to figure out how to get to it," Ryland said.

"That is what we're doing now," Essa explained.

He shook his head. "If you look up the Tree of Life in the Bible, it talks of getting though many obstacles before arriving at it, a pearl gate, and the Tree being protected by angels possessing swords of fire."

"Just as I taught in my last class, God uses signs because that is how our brain is wired. We are also chemical. So that may be a portion of things, too."

"Isn't that going too far?" Amana asked.

"Not really." Essa uncrossed her legs. "Look at how doctors have studied how the brain changes when someone is focused in prayer or worship."

"Why a tree?" Amana asked.

"For one thing, Jesus died on a tree," Essa said.

Ryland walked over to the easel and started to draw. "I was

researching the northwest islands, and it is a great location for the Tree of Life. Those are the oldest in the chain. They are gradually being reclaimed be the sea. The tectonic plate they are on slid over a volcanic hotspot seventy million years ago, which built them up from the ocean and created islands. As they continue to shift away, they sink." He tapped the marker on the paper. "Most of them are atolls now. So it would make sense to look in the water for the Tree as there is little land left. Being so old, it may have gradually adapted to thriving in salt water."

"A symbol God uses for baptism is water," Essa added.

"But the swords of fire couldn't exist under water," Amana said.

"Or could they?" Ryland raised one brow. "Haven't you ever seen the lava rise from spots in the sea floor?"

"Good line of reasoning," Amana admitted. "Just one moment." She left the room. She returned with a DVD in hand and fed it into the player. "I remembered Planet Care had this in their library. It's on the northwest islands, and I think we should view what we'll encounter."

Scenes of a sandy oasis appeared on the screen. The narrator began. "This rare and fragile coral ecosystem lies across 1,200 miles of the Pacific Ocean. The area is called Papahanaumokuakea by native Hawaiians, but one thousand years ago, their ancestors called it home. Several of their stone tablets still stand as places of their worship." A helicopter captured aerial pictures of the beautiful atolls. "They are home to seven thousand species of fish, birds, and other animals that include the endangered monk seals. This island chain also provides a place for sea turtles and albatrosses to nest. The National Oceanic and Atmospheric Administration, otherwise known as NOAA, conducted research that helped to provide us with insight into the behaviors of the creatures living there."

Amana checked her watch. "I have a tour coming in half an hour, and I need to get ready. Let's convene for now."

Light between the Leaves

"I have one more question. If we find the Tree, whether above or below, what do we do?" Ryland asked.

Essa sighed. "That is something God has yet to reveal, but I believe it's connected with His purpose He has for each of us."

"Let's come back tonight and plan our adventure." Amana jiggled keys in her hand.

They gathered their belongings, and Amana locked the door.

Essa saw Hugh strutting down the hall, whistling a tune. He gave a quick smile, saluted them, and passed on to his office.

Chapter 12

Amana met two families visiting from Colorado. They hiked through bifurcating nature trails and up winding paths in the mountains. She led them up an untamed pass where three waterfalls melded. She thought about her late grandpa. What did he do when he served? Was he there when Midway was bombed?

Her stomach gurgled. They had picnicked at the water feature around eleven, but it was now well into the afternoon. She guided the group back to the Range Rover and gave them time to settle their children in their seats. She rang her aunt.

'Akau answered at once.

"I'm going over to Grandma Meli's to bring her some dinner, and I wanted to see if you would like to come, too."

"I have a meeting at four, and I'm not sure how long it will run. I had better pass."

"Earlier, a friend of mine was telling me about the northwest islands, and it reminded me that grandpa was stationed there. I'm curious to hear more about it from grandma."

"Change of plans," her aunt interrupted. "I will make it to her house for dinner. I'll see you in an hour."

Amana stood in confusion. Her Aunt 'Akau, the district attorney, was going to cancel her meeting? She wondered what changed her mind. What would make her drop important business to meet for a simple meal?

Amana stopped by the market and grabbed some precooked mahi-mahi, wine, cheese, and berries. She packed it in a basket lined with tea towels and drove to her grandma's house. The fencing Grandpa Noah had put up decades ago looked the same. Several times Aunt 'Akau paid to have the house repainted, and each time, grandma insisted on keeping it the same color it had always been. Grandma's main pride was in the yellow flowers she tended that lined the driveway.

Amana knocked on the door and entered without waiting. She kept a clean home, but often forgot to dust. A layer sat atop of the microwave and fridge. Amana placed the basket of food on the kitchen table.

"Grandma Meli, where is your cleaning rag?"

Meli pointed to the cabinet below the sink. Amana took some cleaning spray and wiped in slow strokes. Aunt 'Akau walked into the room and embraced Amana tightly.

"Everything will be just fine" 'Akau told her.

Amana stepped back and tilted her head. "What are you talking about?"

Grandma Meli took her by one hand and led her into the living room. 'Akau hurried behind them.

Meli sat her granddaughter in the middle of the couch. "We have a bit of a story to tell." She reached for the beads of Amana's bracelet and twisted them between her fingers. "This was a gift."

"Yes, I remember Auntie having it for years, and then when I turned eighteen, she gave it to me."

Her grandma's eyes twinkled. "It has been passed down. Grandpa Nohakai gave it to me when we were first married."

Only Meli called him Nohakai. Everyone else called him Noah. But that was her grandma, always precise.

'Akau leaned in closer. "She gave this to you because it was time."

Grandma Meli stopped caressing the beads and took Amana's hand. "When your grandfather enlisted in the navy, he was sent to Midway Atoll in the northwest islands. One assignment in particular had him diving somewhere off the coast of Sand Island. He wasn't used to the current out there, and two of them were converging. He started to drown. That is when an angel appeared to him, plain as day, and saved him." Grandma Meli adjusted her glasses. "When they got him out of the water, the Navy wrote it off as a near death experience, or NDE."

She lifted the beads away from Amana's wrist. "He had the thorns of an acacia clasped tightly in his hand. He held onto them for days before he'd let his fingers release. He told me what heaven was like." Her mouth curved upward, encased in a tender memory. "When he wrote me from the island, he described what happened. The angel took him to the Tree of Life, and he traveled through a tunnel. He saw the bright light." She took a sip of her wine.

"I dismissed it as a traumatic experience. But when he came home to me, he had made this bracelet out of the thorns from that tree." She sniffled back a tear and cleared her throat before continuing. "He said God had asked him to protect the area, and he had accepted that responsibility. That is why those islands are only used for ecological values and maintained mostly free of people—because of his promise he kept to our Lord. If it ever got in the wrong hands, it could destroy a covenant."

Aunt 'Akau added. "Since your grandpa's passing, I've been taking care of the legislation to keep those islands and atolls protected. It is now your turn, Amana."

"How am I supposed to do that?"

"God will lead you."

"Grandpa described it as a passage?" Amana asked.

"Tunnel." Grandma Meli corrected her.

"My friends have chartered a plane and dive boat to take us out there. Did Grandpa say exactly where this was?"

"No," Grandma Meli said, shaking her head. "He said it was better if he had not. It sounds like the Lord is trying to lead you and your friends to that site for a specific reason. Amana, I've never had the privilege of seeing the Tree." She paused a moment, staring at the beads and lost in a memory. "You know that Hawaiian names have meanings. My name means 'honey bee.' When you are out there searching for the Tree, I will pray for the Holy Spirit to help guide you on your journey. When you see a honey bee, you'll know you are close."

Chapter 13

Essa returned to her apartment. A red light blinked on her answering machine. She checked the caller ID and saw Willa's name. I'll call her back, she thought and looked at her laundry basket of clean clothes sitting on the bed. She folded them carefully and smoothed them out to avoid ironing. The heap of dishes piled in the sink needed cleaning, too. Looking out the window while doing the dishes, she thought of Ryland. Was he flirting with her on the beach the night before? When she first met Ryland, she was excited by his presence. His wide smile gleamed warmth from his soul. She was filled with anticipation of seeing him again. The next time she saw him was in her class. Her heart sank, knowing that an arm's-length friendship was the only rapport they would have. Now that grades were turned in, she could anticipate something more. Somehow the idea of a deeper relationship made her nervous.

She stopped by the church to weed the flower beds around the building. The shed behind the building contained gardening tools, and she took out what she would need. She pulled the cotton gloves over her knuckles. They were caked with dried

Light between the Leaves

mud. She knelt on a foam board and tugged the stalks of grass and weeds from freckled purple orchids and hues of red hibiscus. There in the ground, she saw the trace of a thick curve between two shrubs, maybe marking something important.

She got up and walked into the church office to ask. Pastor Gill was at the receptionist's computer, typing his next sermon.

He peered over his thin framed glasses. "Our flowers are so grateful you came today!" he said.

"I saw an unusual shape in the soil, so I thought it best not to disturb that area."

"Oh? Let's go take a look."

They walked back to the place, and he bent over to look at the curvature. He laughed when he saw what she had found. "This must be from Taylor. She plants, fertilizes, and weeds on the days you had class." He motioned for Essa to come closer. "In the first century A.D., the Ichthus, or a drawing of a fish, was a Latin sign. Christian travelers would draw half of this fish in the dirt, and if another person venturing along the same road was a follower of Jesus Christ, they would draw the other half."

Essa took her finger and finished the picture.

"Next time Taylor is out here, she'll see this and know you responded as her sister in Christ."

Essa returned home to take a shower before heading to the college and then to finish their meeting at Planet Care. She went to her closet to put on the sundress she had bought when she arrived in Honolulu. It had dark green material and delicate white lace around the straps and heart-shaped front.

When she arrived at the university soon after, she stopped at the human resource department.

"I need a permit application to research in the monument." Essa told the receptionist.

The woman handed her a form and pen, and she took a seat in the bustling lobby. She marked the category as research and noted that the vessel had already been approved since the charter service was already taking a group out there.

She read the quick blurb on prohibitions: no oil or gas exploration, no releasing of a new species or anchoring on the coral. The form gave her about two inches to provide an abstract detailing her investigation and explained that she would have to distribute her findings within thirty days of the trip. Essa turned it in, and the woman assured her she would receive a slip in her faculty mail box if it was approved or denied.

That done, Essa continued on to Planet Care. Her bike tires skidded to a halt in the dusty lot. The colors of the sunset swirled in the breezy sky. Rain began to patter on her head. She ran into the building and to the front desk where she found Amana stacking up release forms.

"I'm waiting on Ryland." Amana's eyes hung heavy.

"Long day?"

"Since Hugh began his position here, he has had me out of the office scouring the island for new excursion sites."

"Where is he?"

"He left for the day."

Essa looked out the large front window and saw Ryland pull up on his moped.

He walked in carrying his helmet under his arm.

"I'm glad you made it," Amana said. "I'll get the keys for the board room." Amana opened the drawer and produced a large silver key ring. The keys chimed when she walked. Essa and Ryland followed her down the empty hallway single file.

She unlocked the door and opened it. Essa waited outside for her to find the light switch. Their paper notes had been scattered around the room as if a tornado had whipped through.

Essa's eyes grew as she followed the thrashed trail to the easel. The markers were tossed around the floor and the rolled paper they had written clues on had been ripped off and taken.

A jagged edge was the only remnant of the list of clues they had compiled.

"What happened?" Ryland asked Amana.

Her face wrinkled as she examined the mess. "I don't know. This room has been locked since we last left it."

"Did you leave those keys in the drawer when you went out today?" Essa asked.

"Yes, but who would do this?" Amana shifted her gaze between her friends. "Visitors don't know where I keep them."

Ryland walked across the floor and began picking up papers.

Essa placed her hand over her forehead. "Our research is compromised." She rubbed the shivers growing over her arms. She glanced up at Amana. "Do you think Hugh was angry we used this room for personal reasons?"

"I doubt it. When he saw us leaving this morning, he had a genuine smile on his face and has seemed happy the whole day." Her voice cracked with strain. "I even heard him whistling from his office in the back of the building."

"Who would know we were here and what we were doing?" Essa asked, not expecting an answer.

Amana shook her head.

"Oh, no." Essa put her hand over her mouth. "Willa called me last night. She said she didn't want to tell me before but it had been weighing on her mind."

"What about?" Ryland was quick to inquire.

"She overheard Dean Sterns talking to some guy about buying out the botany program for land the university owns. I don't know what else it entailed. Do you think someone has been following me?"

Ryland stood up with the pile of papers and placed them on the table. "What would they want with information about a *potential* tree?"

"If the person behind all this finds the Tree before we do, they could take possession of it. It could become the next world wonder." She rubbed her face. "If that were to happen, people would flock from around the world, and the whole area would go to ruins!"

Amana nodded, understanding the disaster that would cause. "Right now it's protected, but it is difficult enough for people to keep cleaning up the mess from trash brought in by currents."

"Sure," Essa said, "if the botany program is awarded any grants for substantial research I have done, then it will bring more money to the university so they'll be less willing to sell the land."

Amana cleared her throat. "Wouldn't the dean only consider selling it if he was put between a rock and a hard place?"

"I don't know." Essa sighed and looked around the room. "Someone has our research information and probably intends on using it. I wonder if God want us to continue looking for the Tree?"

"Go to the Bible and ask Him." Amana pointed to the Bible left untouched on the far table.

Essa closed her eyes and went silent in prayer. She took the Bible and opened it. Her eyes rested on Ezekiel 48:14. " 'They must not sell or exchange any of it. This is the best of the land and must not pass into other hands, because it is holy to the Lord.' "

Amana smiled, "Yes, I think God heard your plea." This guided confidence from the Lord calmed her fear. She was ready to tell her friends about her grandpa's secret.

Growing footsteps echoed on the tile floor in the hallway. Amana's eyes grew.

The door flung open, and Essa gasped at who she saw. Camille, Essa's younger sister, was probably the last person she expected to show up, yet it was her. Camille stood in a camouflaged tank top and army green pants. Her sandy blond hair frizzed wildly around her body like a swarm of flies. She looked at her sister and said, "What? It's like you're staring at a ghost."

Essa grabbed her hand. "Camille, what are you doing here? You scared the life out of me!"

"Musta' been an intense moment." She chuckled and dropped

her luggage. "Just got off the plane. I stopped by your office, but some guy said you might be here." She took a chair, swung it around, and sat backwards. She rested her chin on her hands. "Happy to see me?"

"I'm in shock." Essa shook her head. "Why didn't you call?"

"Not my style."

Essa closed her eyes and took a deep breath. "Ryland, Amana, please forgive me, but my sister and I have a bit of catching up to do."

"Of course." Amana attempted a smile but the concern was evident on her arched brow. This wasn't good timing. "We'll take our remaining notes to a safer place."

Chapter 14

Essa led Camille outside Planet Care. "Where's your ride?"

"I took a taxi from the airport." Camille looked around the empty parking lot. "Where's yours?"

"I just have a ten-speed bike. My apartment is three miles from here! I guess we're walking." Essa hit the kickstand and guided the bike alongside her sister.

They walked in silence for a few minutes until Essa couldn't stand it.

"Camille, what are you doing here?"

"I came to see you."

"I haven't heard from you in almost a year. You didn't even come to say goodbye before I left for Hawaii."

"I'm here now."

"*Why* now?" Essa wanted a shred of understanding.

"Being out in the middle of nowhere doesn't allow me to keep in communication as often as the technological world does."

"You mean like telephones?"

"Have you ever tried to get reception on the rapids? That's why I don't even bother owning a cell." She slurped her drink.

"It's not like there's an outlet to plug a computer in when camping along the rivers, either."

"That's no life to lead. Why don't you just come home?"

"Why don't you?"

"I moved all the way out here for a job, money. Something in the field I've been working toward for the past six years, Camille."

"And being a rapids guide is my job."

"Are you going to do that forever?"

"I realize it is not what you want to do, but I'm a different person than you are, Essa. It doesn't make it wrong." Her voice cracked.

Essa placed her hand on Camille's. "You're right, and I'm sorry. I don't understand. I've had to justify to people why I don't know much about my own sister. I've felt like you've been running away from your family."

Camille turned to face Essa. "Mom and dad only listen to me if I have great news, so when I call, I rarely tell them about my life." She fanned herself. "Grandma Rose, on the other hand, is the only one that understands me."

"You two seem to be close."

"There's a reason." Camille paused. "The more I think about it, the more I gotta wonder if Mom ever told you. Like I said, she only talks about things if they're good, and Dad just doesn't say much of anything."

"It's not terrible to talk about wonderful things."

"Nope, but it promotes misunderstandings. I came out here because Grandma Rose knew I could help you."

Essa turned to look at her. "With what? I'm doing fine on my own," she asked.

"It looks like it from the sight of that meeting room."

Essa rolled her eyes.

Camille didn't say anything for a moment. Essa saw that she was struggling to find her words. They walked silently for the next hundred yards.

"I carry around a lot of guilt," Camille finally said.

"Why, what did you do?" This was getting confusing.

"We were all at Grandma Rose's one day, playing out in the backyard. Gosh, we were so young, probably five and seven years old? I had to come in to pee."

Essa sighed at Camille's choice of words.

"I found her crying over an ultrasound picture in her hand. She tried to hide it, but not before I read the two baby names typed across the front."

"Who were they?" Essa didn't remember a family member having twins.

"Mom was carrying two of us." She raised her head, attempting to stop the flow of tears that had suddenly started. "My twin failed to grow. She was stillborn. Since then, I've carried guilt around for being the one spared." She stopped to sniff hard and wipe her nose. "I made it my point in life to live it to the fullest and live it for the life she didn't have."

Essa stopped in the middle of the road. She turned Camille by the arm and looked straight at her. "I had no idea. No one told me." Soon, the tears pooled in her eyes, too.

"That's what I figured. It took me years to realize why I was living the way I was. I finally sought a counselor who helped me sort it out."

Essa wondered why she didn't know. That kind of thing does not usually remain a secret in family circles for long. How was this one kept?

"Grandma Rose promised to never tell a soul and leave that up to mom. Grandma and I are so close because she is the only one that understands me. I can tell her when I'm having a bad day, and she listens."

"Why did you wait so long to tell me? That must have been terrible carrying that around."

"You and Blaise are so similar; I guess I wanted to keep our sister to myself."

The words 'our sister' hit Essa's heart and slammed it into the back of her rib cage.

"Now tell me why I walked into that torn apart room at Planet Care." She stretched her arms, "and I don't want to hear that it was a window you left open. The truth."

Essa found herself pouring out the details of the past semester.

"I'm going with you," Camille replied. "Not only am I a technical certified diver, but my survival skills are pretty impressive." She laughed.

Essa's jaw quivered, and Camille pulled her sister to her and hugged her tight.

Essa struggled to speak. "We have so much time to make up for."

When they arrived at the apartment building, Essa went around to unlock the door. She dropped her purse and turned on the lamp next to the couch. "Just leave your luggage in my bedroom." She walked into the kitchen and put the kettle under the faucet. "Do you want some tea?"

"That sounds good." Camille shouted from the sofa.

They took their cups out to the patio and sat watching the ocean.

Chapter 15

Ryland checked the written slip of paper. "Building three," he whispered to himself in the dimly lit marina. He approached the metal-rippled boat house with hesitation. The only lights came from the lamp posts lining the docks. The air was silent except for the gentle sound of water lapping against the sides of boats. No cars were parked outside, and he contemplated whether he had gotten the right location.

He pushed hard on the glass door, expecting it to give resistance. It swung open fast and left Ryland to fall. He was quick to catch himself and regained his composure.

The front office was desolate and dark. He scanned for an entry connecting it to the back of the place. He hurried to a closed wooden door and found a bathroom. He saw an inconspicuous opening at the far end. It was another door left ajar. He walked through it and into the main portion of the building.

Hushed whispers came from behind a row of pontoon boats poised high on trailers. Ryland approached with caution. A large shadow outlined Bockman's body shape.

"Ah, there's my protégé!" Bockman called to Ryland. "Hugh,

let me introduce you to my intern, Ryland Baines. Ryland, this is Hugh."

They shook hands.

"I've seen you at Planet Care with Amana and Essa. Great work acting as one of them."

Ryland shrugged and smirked.

"When we land this acquisition, I'll be moving Ryland up to associate," Bockman told Hugh and smiled knowingly.

Hugh placed his hands in his dress pants pockets. "Why did you mess the room up? All you needed to do was get the information."

"That was my suggestion," Bockman added. "I wanted to terrify them."

"That seems to have hurried their pace," Hugh replied.

"Where is the research information?"

Ryland pulled out the papers he had gathered from the board room that night and handed them to his boss.

Bockman compared the clues that had been written on the rolled paper and tried to make sense of them. He shared the papers with Hugh.

"Sorry about the lack of lighting," Hugh apologized. "I couldn't take the chance of having our meeting in my new office. We wouldn't want Amana coming in and seeing us with Ryland."

Bockman added, "Stupid girls. They have no idea he's with us. It makes it all the easier to acquire their secrets." He released a bellowed laugh. "Looks like they're intent on searching for this tree. You know," he tapped the paper with his index finger, "we could use this as a great marketing ploy to bring people into the resort."

Hugh smiled broadly. "Free tours while staying on the grounds. The whole world will jump at the chance to see the one and only Tree of Life."

Bockman closed his eyes. "I see the dollar signs already. We'll let the girls do all the work and follow closely behind."

Hugh turned to Ryland. "Keep being a *friend* to them. I don't want them the wiser, got it?"

Ryland nodded. A dull ache pulled at his heart. The more he received the word of God, the more it happened, his conscience telling him to turn away. How could he hurt Essa? He didn't sign up for all this deception when he was hired at Bockman's firm. He was pulled into it, and it became harder to see the truth. He felt like a cartoon character that had an angel on one shoulder and the devil on the other. I'm a saved Christian, he thought. How did I end up on this side of the tracks?

Ryland knew he had turned the other cheek too many times and had made deliberate choices to do so. He hated himself for that and tried to remind his heart that this was the only time he'd need to do this. All I have to do is follow the girls, and then it will end, and I can go on with my life.

"You'll get a cozy corner office when you bring in this fish," Bockman said with a wink.

"How's Stern's coming?" Hugh asked.

"He's on board as long as we can ensure Essa doesn't publish any findings. We need to claim them. Sterns just wants to retire. It helps that the previous botany professor had not done a lick of research or applied for any grants. The pressure rests on Essa, but her plans are going to work for us."

"Sounds good," Hugh said. "What's next in the game plan?"

Ryland answered him. "According to her clues, she believes the Tree lies in the northwest archipelago somewhere. She already booked the plane and chartered a boat at Midway."

"No worries, Ry. We'll be following." Bockman pulled a cell phone out of his back pocket and handed it to him. "This phone has a global tracking device. Keep it with you at all times."

Ryland nodded, and his guilt set in. These girls did not deserve to lose their careers. "Promise me no one will get hurt."

"Of course not. Our goal is to acquire land, not bodies," Bockman said with a shocked look. "Who do you think I am?"

Light between the Leaves

Camille had stopped by the dive shop to pick up the wetsuits, buoyancy control vests, and regulator rentals. She had requested the fins, masks, tanks, and weights be included on the boat. Camille had bought a new dive computer and turned it on to check its working order. She pivoted in a circle. The compass was stuck on northwest. She shook it gently, and it corrected the bearings.

Essa had packed light for the journey. They would only be gone for two days. She shoved a few sweat shirts for any cool nights on the boat. She placed her Bible, notes, and map in her purse, wheeled the luggage to the door, and called for a taxi.

Ryland arrived first and helped the cabbie lift the bags into the trunk. Camille had picked up Amana on the way back from the dive shop. The girls preoccupied themselves with conversation.

Ryland wondered whether Bockman were close. He looked in all directions and sensed they were being watched. His eye caught a light gray sedan parked down the hill. A man with jet black hair and a matching thick beard exited the driver's door. He rested his back against the side and examined a large paper. The strong sun illuminated the top half of a concealed gun tucked in the man's jeans.

Ryland squinted and wondered whether that was Bockman in disguise. Bockman had promised that no one would get hurt. If that was him, why was he carrying a pistol?

The girls arranged themselves in the vehicle, and Ryland sat in the passenger seat. The taxi driver pulled away from the curb. Ryland leaned to his side and checked the rearview mirror. The man down the block was out of view. He sat back in his seat and chewed his finger nail. He popped over and looked again. The car was directly behind them now. He reminded himself that it didn't mean it was him. He whispered to the driver, "Make a sharp left at the next street."

The taxi driver shot him a confused expression and swerved the vehicle. The other car delayed for a moment and, in an exaggerated curve, turned with them. Ryland sat down and sighed a heavy breath. His cell phone rang several times in a row.

It caught the attention of the girls in the back. "Answer that, Ry. It's beginning to drive me nuts," Camille told him.

He hit the answer button and listened.

"Don't pull any tricks or one of you won't make it back home." The phone went silent.

It was him. This was too much. He knew he had made wrong choices, but this was something he did not want any part of. Should he warn the girls? He rummaged his brain for a plan. Maybe he could alert them to the possibility without scaring them.

He twisted his body to face the back seat. "What if the same people who ransacked the board room decide to follow us?"

"Have you gone mad?" Essa asked. "How would they know when we were leaving?"

"Look, just don't underestimate bad people."

She pulled some lip gloss out of her purse and swiped it across her lips. "We have nothing to worry about."

"Don't you remember what Willa had warned?"

She rolled her eyes and looked at the ocean out the window.

Amana adjusted in her seat. "I was going to tell you all something the night Camille showed up, but I didn't get the chance." A smile rounded out her full cheeks. She proceeded to divulge the story about Grandpa Noah. She gave every detail, from his drowning to the angel's visit and near death experience at the Tree of Life.

Essa reacted visably. "I realize that we're seeing God's guidance manifest as tangible evidence. It is just so, so . . . ."

Amana placed her hand on Essa's shoulder. "There is still disbelief in our hearts."

Essa sucked in a quick breath. "Yes." She lowered her eyes. "I just wonder about all this. My faith is supposed to be full and all believing. I wonder if we can do this, if I can do this, when I lack the main element of devotion."

Amana continued, "I know we were thinking it might also be on land, but because of this, I have more reason to believe it is in the waters near Midway Atoll." She unraveled her map on the car seat. "There are several small islands and shoals around it. We can't even make an educated guess as to where to start."

"We need a sign from God. Put faith first and the rest will follow." Essa was determined to show God that she accepted His truths and was willing to be an agent to help connect others to Christ.

The pilot stood in the open door of the high-speed Learjet 60. A ladder stretched to the concrete. He greeted each of his passengers and had them pile their luggage in the front. He secured the netting to keep the baggage in place. They had to duck in the plane's shallow interior. Shiny wood trim lined the sides, and the seats were dressed in soft beige leather.

"Exactly how much did you pay for these plane tickets, Essa?" Amana asked. "We don't require luxury."

"It is a bit much, I guess. I expected a puddle jumper with non-reclining metal seats imbedded with the smell of must." She ran her hands over the sheepskin armrests.

Ryland tilted his chair and wiggled into a comfortable position.

They sat in a humid heat. "What are you doing," Essa asked Ryland. "Not scared to fly, are you?"

"My shorts are beginning to stick to the seat. I think they need to check the air conditioning."

Essa glanced out the tiny window. The fog on it outlined an image. She lazily traced her finger along it. "Look!" She got Amana's attention. "It's a honey bee."

Amana leaned across Essa's lap. "That's a sign."

"What sign?" Essa asked.

"The one you said we needed from God."

"How is the image of a honey bee a sign?" Essa asked her.

"My grandma said to follow the bee. This will lead us to where the Tree of Life is." She tapped Essa on the hand. "Don't you see? God is confirming our suspicion."

Essa looked back at the image, dumbfounded. "Honey bees hover above land, not the ocean. I still say we need to look on some of the islands."

"I'll keep my eyes open," Camille replied.

"That will be helpful," Amana said with a knowing smile.

They sat for another half hour. "I wonder what is taking so long," Ryland said.

"I'll go ask the captain." Camille walked up front and tapped on the pilot's door. He opened it to let her in. He had his head phones on and was monitoring several dials.

"When is take off, cap?"

"We're waiting for a replacement."

"You're not flying us there?"

"Guess not," he said. "Means I've got the rest of the day off. I'll get to take the kids to t-ball with my wife instead of spending a few days in the middle of nowhere."

"When is the other pilot supposed to get here?"

"A few minutes, I think."

Camille went back to her seat. A light gray car pulled parallel to the plane. The girls tried to gain a glimpse of the replacement pilot, but all they could see was a thick head of dark hair. The cabin door shut, and the first pilot left down the stairs.

The propellers churned, and the engine hummed. Essa looked out her window to see that they were taxiing down the runway. Ryland's phone buzzed.

"Hey," Camille said. "You've got to shut that off so it doesn't interfere with the communication of the radio tower."

"Yeah, I will. Just let me read this text." His eyes glanced over the words; 'Come to the cockpit.' He did not understand, and then it dawned on him. *No, this can't be right.*

He tore off his seat belt and took long strides down the aisle. He knocked on the door, and it cracked open. He entered the cockpit and sat in the empty seat next to the man. Bockman stared back at him and ripped off his wig and fake beard.

"What do you think you're doing?" Ryland asked.

"I will not let anything or anyone get in my way of acquiring that land."

"Do you even know how to fly a plane?"

"I got my license years ago, but I still remember." He frowned at Ryland. "You underestimate me."

Ryland wanted out of this deal—now. The pressure had been building, and he was cornered. He had to call it off with Bockman. Of course, he certainly couldn't do it right then.

"I saw the gun on your side." He shook his head. "This is out of control. You can't go around following people and threatening them."

"I'm not threatening them. It's a promise," Bockman said. He looked over the dials for a moment, holding up one hand for Ryland to be quiet. He nodded at what he saw on the panel, and then turned back to Ryland. "What are you gonna do, fight me? You don't know how to fly this thing, Ryland. You have no choice *but* to trust me." He laughed with confidence.

Ryland pursed his lips. He balled his fists, hating the control that Bockman had over him. He felt like a caged rabbit. He wanted desperately to turn away from the bad and run to God. He was in too deep with the devil. But he had to wonder, was he still worth saving? He didn't know.

He silently admitted defeat, and returned to his seat. He closed his eyes and prayed in his head. *"God, I know I'm not worthy. I've made so many bad choices, but I don't want that kind of life. I don't want people to get hurt because of me. Please help us all. Help us land safely and defeat this evil. I need you more than ever, God. Please hear me."* He opened his eyes to find Essa staring at him.

"You didn't answer me," she said.

"I didn't hear you. What did you say?"

"I asked why you went up to the cockpit."

"I wanted to find out if I could get a free wing pin," he lied.

More lies! God, I want to stop! He cried out in his head.

Chapter 16

The sleek jet shook as it slowed in preparation to land. The miniature runway of Sand Island of the Midway atoll came into view, and soon they were on the ground. When the plane stopped, they gathered their belongings. Ryland tapped on the pilot's door. "Are you gonna drop the ladder, or am I?"

No one answered. He took hold of the lock, pulled the handle, and released them. He wondered why Bockman had not kidnapped them all while he had the chance. Ryland ventured to guess he needed them to lead him to the Tree of Life, but he would be close by.

What would he do if they did find it? Ryland's memory went back to seeing the flash of sunlight on Bockman's pistol. He pleaded with God to make a possibility for a way out, an escape from this lunatic and his own chance to step out of the darkness and start living in the light with other Christians.

They exited the plane in the salted ocean wind. The flat island was green with shrubbery and was encircled with a narrow strip of white beach. Constant obnoxious chattering resounded from hundreds of birds that had made Midway their nesting site.

Essa glanced toward the interior of the island. Many remnants from WWII had remained, a storage bunker, pill box, and a huge free-standing machine gun. A curious two-story building had been long abandoned. White paint chipped from its exterior. The windows were outlined in a blue border that had been bleached by the intense sun.

Laysan albatrosses floated on the restless gusts. They maneuvered landings among the tree branches and waddled across the grass to regurgitate their recent finds to their chicks. Two attempted to impress a female by their clucking, cawing, and mating dances. They mirrored each other with their neck stretches. Essa turned her head toward the water.

The owner of the dive boat stood on the grassy shore next to a yellow inflatable dinghy with paddles sticking out its side. She greeted him and promised to have the boat back in a day.

The white vessel was moored in ten feet of reef-filled water. Ryland recognized it as the one they had seen anchored at the Oahu marina.

Scuba tanks were secured by bungee cords and lined the sides of the boat's interior. They boarded eagerly. They strapped their buoyancy control vests to the tanks and sat on the metal bench. Amana had climbed the short ladder to the deck and checked the sonar head and steering. She yelled down below. "We're equipped with DAN oxygen units and first aid kits."

"That's a plus," Ryland shouted back to her over the engine noise. "We might need those, especially since this will be a place none of us has ever dived before."

Amana started up the short ladder to the cabin. "I'll check the radio for the currents," she told Ryland

Everything was in working order. They waved to the dive operator and headed for sea.

Amana drifted the boat past several atolls of the archipelago. Sandbars peeked out of the turquoise waters with occasional sheer rock formations on island outcrops.

Essa searched for one with vegetation higher than shrubbery.

Light between the Leaves

She spotted a mature forest in the distance and asked Amana to get closer. Amana headed the boat in toward its direction and cut the motor to drift around the sudden shallow boarder. The trees posted themselves off the beach.

"Coast in, and we'll pull up enough to anchor in the sand," Essa instructed her. She took her flip flops off and dangled them from her fingers. Ryland offered a hand to Essa, and she jumped over the hull into the shallow water. They secured the vessel on the shore speckled with marine debris. Plastic bottle caps, a toothbrush, fishing lures, and a golf tee were only a small portion of the trash she saw.

"Look at all this junk!" Amana said, hands on her hips. "I cannot believe there is evidence from humans in the middle of the ocean!"

"I read somewhere that four-fifths of this trash comes from the mainland. The rest is from ships," Ryland added.

"But how does it all get out here?" Essa asked.

"The currents bring it through, and most of it gets trapped in the massive gyre. The birds can fly a far distance from the islands and carry it back to their chicks," Amana explained.

"What's a gyre?" Essa asked.

"A gyre happens when the water rotates in a spiral motion. It's due to the planet spinning and the circulation of the wind." When they looked at her, mouths open, Amana said, "I learned about this from a local fisherman."

"Check this out." Ryland was poking a feathered object with a stick. The carcass of a sea bird shifted along the waves. The half decomposed body revealed pieces of plastic refuse. Camille stepped closer and saw part of a comb, a toy soldier, clothes pin, and a cigarette lighter where the bird's stomach had been.

Amana made a disgusted face and turned her head. "This has to change."

Essa nodded in agreement. "I see why you work in eco-tourism."

"I had better stay with the boat, just in case," Camille said.

"I don't want to finance a stolen vessel for the next twenty years." She ran back. Ryland agreed.

They ambled toward the tree line and took inventory of plants that resembled a variety of familiar species. A few were completely unidentifiable. Essa grasped a serrated leaf in her open hand. "This is a fan palm," she told them. Several shrubs burrowed in the cracks of coral covered by shallow pools. One had snared an old fishing net.

Amana heard grunts and squinted down the beach. Monk seals were nursing their pups. She pointed. "We need to stay clear of them. The mamas can be aggressive."

They walked into the thickets toward the center of the island. The heard the chirp of a repetitive two-note harmony.

Ryland stopped and asked, "What's that noise?"

Amana drew closer to the sound. She looked through the leaves. A gigantic cricket leapt toward her. She screamed and caught her breath with a laugh. "Did you see the legs on that?"

Essa's eyes widened and she quickly looked around. "It makes me wonder what else is in here with us."

"I think these atolls are too small for wild hogs, but if I do see one, I'll be more than happy to save you." Ryland grinned at Essa.

"That's it. I'm going back to the boat," Amana declared.

"Ryland will protect you, too. Won't you?" She jabbed her elbow into his side.

Amana shook her head and said, "I trust Camille to ward off would-be attackers better than the two of you. You and your sister are no way alike." She hiked back toward the coastline and yelled, "Camille is tough. She's like the Joan of Arc of our time."

Ryland waved her off.

Essa took another step and sank to her ankles in the mucky substrate. She lifted a leg and shook the grit. A splat landed on Ryland's cheek. He blinked in surprise and wiped it away with his fingers. "I'm thinking we should've brought a change of clothes."

She peered up the bark on a few small trees. Finches flew

Light between the Leaves

in, out, and around the branches. Above the trees, swarms of sea birds cackled, flying about their nesting sites. She tried to lift her leg, but it would not pull free from the mud. "A little help here," she pleaded.

Ryland grasped her by the calf and yanked back and forth. It rose slowly. "I don't think the acacia is imbedded in this stuff."

"Do you realize how nutrient based this is?" Essa asked.

"But a large tree needs its roots planted in stabilized ground," he countered.

She bent down and noticed a hard protrusion under the vegetation. "There is also coral." She looked up. "I think I see a clearing."

He led her around the quicksand, and they made their way to a steep basalt cliff covered with large feathers and white splatters. A clatter of low and high-pitched clicking noises ensued. The volcano remnant housed nests in the crevices. Tiny white heads with curved beaks poked from the nurseries. The adult albatrosses and frigates were too numerous to count. They hovered until they could narrow in on a swift landing. Several were snatching food off the waves below. Their wing span had to reach at least seven feet across.

The albatrosses had nests made into the sand in the shape of a bowl. A mother stood up off her nest to stretch, and a chick tweeted below her. He had black fluff that came to white tipped spikes all over his body. They seemed gentle and did not mind Essa and Ryland's presence.

A flying frigate rotated its eyes ahead and then at Essa. It mapped out a trajectory, and his gaze met hers. It folded its large black wings close to its body, lowered its head, and plummeted toward her.

Ryland noticed the bird breaking from the pack. He ripped his button down shirt off his chest and sheltered it above their heads. He felt the thick webbed feet push on the thin fabric. Essa stumbled across the rocky niches and fell. She lay on her backside, her leg scraped, with blood beading across the scratches.

Ryland took her arm and swooped her up in one motion. They scrambled back into the small forest under protection of the branches. She buried her face in his solid chest, the force of her breath still fierce.

He wrapped his large arms around her, pinning hers to her sides. She steadied her legs and allowed the calming heat from his body to warm hers. She raised her eyes and met his gaze. Primitive emotions arose. His thick lips crushed hers, and she fell limp in his grasp. The warm pressure teased her lips, and she submitted to his kisses. Her eyelids fluttered, but she regained control. She tried to push him away. He responded by holding her more tightly.

"No," she protested. "I can't like you."

He tipped his head back in confusion. "Why is that? If this is because I *was* your student . . . ."

"That's why I kept a distance."

"I'm not anymore. What I mean to say is that I never was." He stopped himself. If he told her the truth, they would never have a chance together. He just wanted to forget what he had done and vowed to make it right from this point forward. He'd quit the company and make an honest living with a different development firm. But she could never know the truth. He couldn't risk losing something so good.

She looked at him from a sideways glance. "Who are you trying to fool?"

"No one." Not anymore, anyway.

"It's true that I'm not your teacher, but there is something . . . Until I know what is in my heart and get it sorted out, I think we should stick to helping each other find where God is leading us."

He placed his hand on the small of her back, and they continued to the beach. "What's that smell?" he asked.

She looked down and saw a piece of molted seal fur. "My bet's on that! Stick your nose over it and see."

He didn't have to lean forward much to confirm it.

Chapter 17

They met up with Camille and Amana on board the boat.

Ryland twirled one of his curls around his finger. "We need to prove the Tree exists if we're ever going to resolve this conundrum."

Essa shook her head. "I was so sure we'd find it on land. Why on earth would God have placed the Tree under water?"

Camille paced. "Wasn't it you, Essa, who said water is symbolic for baptism?"

It started making more sense to Essa. She took a black dry erase marker and scribbled on the white board they used to map their route.

"God is trying to connect with us," Amana added. "My grandpa told Grandma Meli that he went through a tunnel. What if the Tree of Life was the portal or a link to God?"

Essa lifted her sunglasses and rested them on top of her head. "In my class, I explained what the different parts of the Tree stood for." She crossed her arms and rested her chin in one palm. It was her favorite thinking position.

"Jesus was transformed by death on the cross made from a

tree," Ryland said, "but no one knows for sure what type of wood the crucifix was."

"Wouldn't a greater point be what this object stood for, such as a reference to where a transition can occur?" Essa asked.

Ryland stepped closer to her. "God could be referencing His scripture to strengthen our belief. He is guiding us, and only the pure of faith can correlate the two."

Essa looked into Ryland's eyes, stunned at his deep contemplations.

"Here is our location," Amana said. She stood on the ladder and pointed to the board. She had planned their dive while they were conversing. "There's a current that seems calm today. You three are going to descend to about sixty feet. Keep following your compass in the southwest direction that Ryland's compass arrow keeps pointing to. I'll follow your bubbles, and after I see you've inflated the safety sausage, I'll pick you up."

Ryland looked from one to the other, then said, "If any of us get a sign or nudge from God while we're down there, get the others' attention, and we'll follow together."

"It's not like it should be hard to see a huge tree in the middle of our path." Essa sounded more confident than she felt.

They attached the regulators to the tanks and checked them for air flow. They slid their arms into the buoyancy control vests, slipped their fins on, and placed the masks around their necks. They lined up toward the back of the boat. One by one they toddled to the deck and took a giant stride forward. Their heads surfaced, and they made eye contact before submersing into the blue.

Bits of micro-life and debris decreased the visibility. Essa felt as though she were falling through the clouds. Her ears screamed in sharp pain. She rose up a foot, squeezed her nose, and blew. A pop indicated that she had cleared her ears, and she drifted downward. The visibility cleared, and she could see the sandy floor below her. She met the others at the bottom and drifted.

A goliath grouper bellowed a loud woof and swam past them into a cave carved out on the side of the reef. Coral formed a high wall to their right where a cauliflower polyp swayed its dotted purple arms in the current. Long red tentacles palpated the waters from inside a hole. A white spotted hermit crab crawled along the bottom, inhabiting a brown and pink tortoise-patterned shell. Normal sea life. A school of yellow-striped fish shot through the reef, up and around the structures. Essa kept watch for anything that would give a signal they were close to their goal.

Camille snapped her fingers with a thud to get their attention.

Essa turned and saw a prehistoric fish the size of her head. It peered directly at her sister. Essa swam closer and hoped she wouldn't scare it away. It hovered there, allowing them each to get a look at it. It held its mouth ajar, and she could see long, translucent teeth. A thin extremity off its head supported a photophore that radiated a blue light as it moved back and forth.

She recognized it as a deep sea angler. They normally lived in depths of several thousand feet. What on earth was this creature doing in the shallows? She checked her dive computer. It read sixty-eight feet. The fish turned 180 degrees and jetted forward. Camille swam after it. Essa and Ryland followed. She peeked at her compass, and it moved in the same direction Ryland's compass had been stuck at.

Flecks of gold caught Essa's eye. She focused in on the sand and saw a trail of gold leading off to the right. She tapped Ryland on the fin. He turned around, and she gestured to the golden path. He shook his head and pointed forward to the fish. She continued with them.

After several hundred meters, they came to a stone wall. Each gray block was the same rectangular length and width. She figured it had been built by people. She peered in each direction. It seemed to go on for miles. The angler fish had disappeared, and she wondered what they were going to do now. Ryland kicked off to the left of her. She followed him with Camille.

He faced the wall and swam forward. Essa thought he was going to run into the rock. It had appeared to be one unit, but he had found a recess. There was another wall behind the opening, making it look like a continuous structure. They snaked around the labyrinth and came to a ring of bubbling lava. The blasts of heat warned her to keep back. Long tear-drop flames arose several feet above. Small bubbles floated upward and popped.

Camille tapped on her gauges, revealing she only had 700 psi left. They would still need enough air to get through their decompression stop.

Essa nodded to her and gestured upwards with a questioning look. Camille nodded back. They left through the maze and out the other side of the wall. They rose and stopped at twenty feet for three minutes to avoid the bends. Ryland inflated the orange sausage and let it float upwards. They inflated their buoyancy control vests and followed it to the surface.

Essa tore off her mask. "Did you see that?" she shouted in exaltation.

"Aren't you glad we followed the fish instead of the gold trail?" Ryland asked.

"That rock wall is not naturally occurring," Camille added. "I wonder why people did that. Maybe to protect others from the volcanic activity?"

A honey bee zoomed around the group before disappearing from sight. Ryland ducked under the water when he saw the bee.

"That was weird," Ryland said as he surfaced. The others nodded.

"Too bad we didn't find the tree," Essa said.

"We found something, though." Camille heard the churning of the waves from a vessel. She turned and saw Amana driving the boat in the distance. She got closer and waited until the motors were in neutral. Amana reached down to help them onto the boat. She guided them to their seats and twisted the bungees back on the tanks so they could sit there without falling forward.

"Tell me everything!" Amana insisted.

Chapter 18

"What did you see?" Amana blinked excessively. She could tell by their voices they were discussing something exhilarating.

Camille recounted what they had witnessed.

"How did you locate that break in the rock wall?" Essa asked Ryland. "It looked like it was one barrier."

He paused, and then decided to say it. "I prayed." He unclipped his buoyancy control vest and slipped out of it. "I felt God leading me, and I obeyed. There it was, an opening."

"Dead end, might I add. We did not find a tree," Essa admitted.

Amana continued to assist them in removing their fins and masks. "I say we get you all something to eat, relax a bit, and then go over some things." She went to the cooler and handed out water bottles.

"You know, there's supposed to be a new moon tonight," Camille said.

Amana looked up and said, "God uses the heavens as signs. It's typical in the book of Ezekiel and Revelations."

Essa looked skeptical, and said so. "The only way to heaven

is death. I realize your grandpa had a near death experience, but I'm not willing to do that."

"My grandma said that is what the Navy called it. Grandpa told her that he didn't feel any different and did not remember losing consciousness," Amana said and shrugged.

"God has been showing me glimpses of tree branches," Ryland said. "One branch is reaching up, and one is reaching down, forming a connection, both making an effort to unite."

"What is the physical connection to God?" Essa asked, and they were silent for a moment while pondering.

"I've got it!" Camille cried out. "There is something to that." She paced. "In physics, Albert Einstein and his colleague, Nathan Rosen, developed a theory based on general relativity. It is called the Einstein–Rosen Bridge Theory because it describes a configuration that connects two isolated areas of space-time." She pulled over the white board and drew feverishly:

$$ds^2 = -c^2 dt^2 + dl^2 + (k^2 + l^2)(d\theta^2 + \sin^2\theta\, d\phi^2).$$

The rest of them just looked at her blankly. "Ever heard people describe near death experiences? Most of them talk about a tunnel. That is what this is. God lives out of space and time, so He does not have the limitations that we do."

A large wave rocked the boat. Amana grabbed the side of the rail. "That could've been what happened to my grandpa."

Camille continued, "God is also thought to be exotic matter. If He represents exotic matter, which is indefinable to us at the present time, then that idea can be represented as the Casimir Effect."

"He acts as the force drawing the two ends together?" Essa attempted to make sense of it.

"It has never been proven that anything like this exists, of course. Some say it's an optical illusion," Camille said.

Ryland interrupted, saying, "But our limitations are huge. How can we connect?"

"Think of what we are limited by," Camille explained, "then

alter those, such as physics and chemistry. It has been shown that our brains chemically alter when we're in prayer."

"Prayer has got to be part of it," Essa concluded. "Ryland found the opening in the wall after he prayed!"

"I did, but look. This is good and all, but it doesn't help us figure out what to do or why we are doing this."

Essa grabbed her Bible from her bag. "The Lord has so many surprises beyond what we can see that surpass most of our understanding. We ask Him." She flipped the pages to find Second Chronicles 7:14. "He gives us scripture, rhema words, as part of our clues." She followed her finger to the verse. "It says, 'if my people, who are called by my name, will humble themselves and pray and seek my face and turn from their wicked ways, then will I hear from heaven and will forgive their sin and will heal their land.' "

"He is all powerful. Why doesn't He just speak to us? That would be a whole lot easier!" Amana said, growing frustrated.

"That would eliminate faith. He is an awesome father. Instead of convincing or controlling us, He lets us make decisions. Sometimes we'll fall, but that is all part of the learning process."

"We have to hit pavement before we realize how much we need and want Him," Camille added.

Essa glanced at her with surprise. She didn't even know that her sister was Christian. Sadness swept over her for all the years they had lost. Her assumptions had gotten in the way of the truth. She started pulling off her wetsuit. "Camille, I'm heading up front to lie in the sun. Want to come with me?"

"Sure. I'm right behind you."

Together they walked around the side of the boat and lay across the front. A school of flying fish catapulted themselves out of the water and wiggled their back fins against the waves to catch speed. They opened their wings and glided in the air.

"From a distance, they look like dragonflies," Camille remarked. Soon, the warm sun and gentle rock of the waves pulled Essa into a deep sleep.

Essa dreamed that she was lying on the boat, even as she was. A glowing orange light in the distance came closer until it was upon her. She smiled in her sleep and felt its warmth and comfort. It spoke with a deep, echoing tone. "The Lord wants you to come to Him and reason together. Though you sin, repent, and it will be gone. If you are willing and obedient, you will eat the best from the earth. Are you willing?"

"Wake up." Camille shook her.

Essa opened her eyes and stretched her arms and legs.

"You were talking in your sleep."

Essa yawned and turned her head toward her sister who was sitting up. "I don't even remember falling asleep or what I dreamed. What did I say?" She gave a nervous laugh.

"You kept saying, 'Yes.'"

Suddenly it all came back to Essa. Was it an angel? She *had been* willing to do whatever God intended. Before she revealed her dream, she needed to do something. She jumped up. "I'll be right back." Essa ran around to the interior of the boat and down the stairs. She latched the door behind her.

She kneeled in front of the molded seat and prayed. "Dear Lord, please forgive me of my sins. I have put judgment on people and treated them unfairly. With Your help, I will try my hardest to remind myself not to do this and find out who they are inside their hearts. Thank You for Your saving grace! Amen." She returned to Camille and told her dream.

"Let me get this straight. The angel said that you would eat the best from the earth?" Camille repeated.

Essa nodded.

"That directly ties into my theory that your body would need to be chemically altered in order to achieve what God is allowing for us." She squinted against the setting sun.

"Because of our physical limitations . . ." Essa started. "What if I had to let God know I was willing to go through that before He confirmed the next step?"

"I say we revisit that rock wall. We must be doing something right. When we eventually *find* the Tree, we should eat the fruit." Camille slipped on her fins and snorkel gear.

"We can try it," Essa replied.

"But for now, I'm gonna take in some wildlife."

Camille dove into the blue. She could see eighty feet down. Pristine corals bonded to basalt and created varying levels of depth. Milletseed butterfly fish showed off their agility by weaving in and out of crevices. They moved quickly, but their bright yellow bodies were hard to miss. A brilliant blue outlined their eyes and mouth.

Baby pennant fish worked as cleaners for a blue fin trevally. Their graceful black and white stripes and elongated dorsal fin curved to the force of their movements. A banded shrimp came to join the action and get use of his long, skinny arms with small pinchers on the ends.

Camille spotted the tail of a gray reef shark sondering off to deeper water. A mushroom coral caught her eye, and she performed a jack knife dive. She glided her body around it its ovular shape. It looked like thin segments of blown glass. Something that one might see in an art gallery, she thought.

Camille continued blowing bubbles out her nose and rose to the surface. She gave a forceful blast, shooting the water out of her snorkel and dolphin kicked her body back to a swim position to head back down.

Ryland climbed the ladder to the captain's quarters and sat next to Amana at the wheel. He glanced down at Essa. "Do you think love can conquer anything?" he asked her.

Amana knitted her brows. "Call me a realist, but it depends. Give me an example."

"Let's say there are things in someone's past they are not proud of and want to let the other person know that isn't who they are anymore."

"I suppose if that person has changed with no intention of

going back, then it might give the other a sense of security in knowing that."

He contemplated scenarios in his head. He would tell Essa tonight.

Amana glanced at her watch. It was four o' clock. She clapped her hands several times.

Camille lifted her head out of the water.

"What's going on?" Essa asked.

"We need to get some dinner before getting one more dive in tonight."

When Camille climbed in and dried off, they prepared the food and set up plates. The gusts died down, and the sea grew calm. After their meal, they waited for their stomachs to settle before their night dive. Amana and Camille sat below and played cards.

Ryland took Essa's hand in his and led her up the ladder to the top deck of the boat. Essa stood near the edge and leaned against the side of the boat. Ryland came from behind and wrapped his arms around her. She didn't try to push him away this time.

The sun was sinking into the ocean. A rainbow of coral colors swept the skyline in sheets. They silently watched the dusk transition to nightfall. The outline of where the moon should be seen was illuminated only by the light of the stars.

"It's a new moon," Essa noticed.

Ryland recalled Amana making a reference to that. He grabbed her copy of the Bible on the shelf and flipped through to Ezekiel chapter forty-six. "It says the gate of the inner court facing east is to be shut on the six working days, but on the Sabbath day and on the day of the new moon it is to be opened."

"That's tonight," Essa said.

"We may find what we're looking for on this next dive." He sat in the captain's chair and tugged on her sleeve.

She fell onto his lap and placed her arm around his neck to steady herself. Her eyes lowered to his mouth. She gave up any preconceived notions she had and allowed herself to witness the true loving nature of his soul. She sensed the genuine affections he held for her. He leaned toward her lips with his. She kept still for a moment and then met him half way.

When they broke off the kiss, she said, "There, that didn't hurt so much. Did it?"

He chuckled at her. He pulled a tube of Chap Stick out of his pocket and applied it. "I want to show you what's in my heart." He took hold of her and lightly pressed his face to hers, kissing her again, this time with more passion.

She felt a tingle from every nerve fiber in her body. She ran her fingers through the back of his curled hair and lay across his arms. She felt safe and secure. Essa realized this was what she wanted, a *great* love, a love between two people who adored each other's being, respected one another's intellect, and could work as a team to solve life's issues.

He leaned back in the chair and opened his mouth to say something. He sighed.

"What is it?" she asked.

He stared into her face a moment before looking away. "I'm not perfect."

"I never assumed you were," she teased him.

"I've gotten to know you pretty well since we first met on the church bike trip. Your eyes glistened in the sunlight, and even the sweat gliding down your jaw line made me shake. But nothing compares to what I found and who you were inside." He traced the shape of a heart in the palm of her hand.

"You make me laugh, and I kinda' think you're cute." She blushed. "I've seen you worship in church and know what's really in your heart of hearts."

"Do you like what you see?" he asked.

"I do."

"Your personality is vivacious, curious, and you're willing to go the distance for our Savior. I could see myself spending the rest of my life with someone like that."

Her eyes rounded, and she tensed.

"That's why I want to tell you everything. I owe that to you."

"Should I be scared?" She laughed and assumed he was going to confess trivial things. His silence startled her.

He looked at the floor. Essa's brows knitted together, and she took his face in her hands. He lifted his shiny eyes to hers and attempted to force back tears that had welled.

"I got in with the wrong people." Ryland looked up to the sky, obviously not willing to meet her eyes. "Have you ever noticed how difficult it is to the right things when you are in deep?"

She recalled the kindness her sister Camille had given in return for her harsh judgments. In that case, it seemed easy to right the wrong because of grace. Essa wasn't naive enough to suspect this was always the case. She knew it was the exception. That was one of the reasons why the presence of mercy made her so thankful for the healing of their broken relationship.

"I've been forgiven," Essa told him. "Not only by those I've hurt in the past but also by Jesus because He knew I was sincere when I asked Him."

"I'm involved with Bockman."

"What?" Essa leapt off his lap and backed into the corner of the wall.

"Please hear me out."

"No!" She looked back and forth, from him to the ladder down. She wanted to run and tell the girls, warn them, but they were all on the boat together. How could she get away from him? She realized she didn't have a quick solution and stood there listening to his pleas. Essa attempted to block them out, but it didn't work.

"I tried so many times to figure out how to quit." He leaned against the other wall, giving her space. "He is an evil man, Essa. He lures people in, and then places them in situations where it is near impossible to get out. He threatens people and has a gun he carries with him."

"Where is Bockman?"

Light between the Leaves

"I don't know. There was a global positioning system affixed to the business phone he gave me. I tossed it over the cliff on the island to throw him off. I'm hoping that gives us enough time to figure out what we need to."

"How can I trust you? How do I know you aren't using us to find the Tree then hurt us or worse?"

He lowered his head. "I'll tell you how." He came closer to her. She tried to back up further, but then realized she was as far away as she could get. He placed his hands on her shoulders. She shook in fear and wept. She wondered if she should scream.

"Look at me. Just look at me, ok?" He took his finger and wiped her cheek. "I'm not a bad guy. Listen to me, I promise with all my heart and with the help of God, that I will get us all out of this mess." He rolled his eyes. "Just a second ago, you saw into my being and knew the real me."

Her mind raced in confusion. "Please don't hurt me," she begged.

"There is no way I could ever do that," he whispered.

"Essa, are you all right?" Essa heard Amana calling.

Ryland pleaded with his eyes not to give them alarm. She glanced at the ladder and back at him.

"Essa, I asked God for forgiveness. He erased my bad decisions."

"Tell me *everything*, all the secrets!" Essa spoke in a staccato whisper. Her body trembled.

"Essa?" Now Camille was calling.

"We're just talking," Essa replied.

Ryland gave her the whole story, from the first day he went to the interview at the development company to Bockman's scheme involving Hugh and Sterns.

Essa grabbed his shoulders and demanded, "Answer me. Where is Bockman now? His boat may very well be hidden close by us in the darkness and fog."

"They don't know where we are. Like I said, I ditched the cell phone just off the island." She gave him a leery look. "Look for my cell phone, or better yet, call it."

She slid her phone out of her pocket and dialed his number. She couldn't hear a ring, but he could have put it on silence mode.

He handed her his back pack and belongings. "Check these. I've got nothing to hide anymore."

She hesitated and dug through them. Nothing.

"How can I make this better? How can I show you I will never hurt you and I'm on your side?" He encircled her with his muscular arms. His warmth helped her body to stop shaking. He raised her chin and kissed her with an uncommon tenderness. "Can we pray together? I know you trust God with all of your mind and soul. Let Him tell you."

She felt an urging from her Holy Spirit to pray with him. She nodded in slow motion. He took her hands in his, and they bowed their heads. "Our God, Father of creation, the wicked cannot dwell with you. Keep us safe and away from any evil. Protect each of us and reveal the truth. Deliver us from the enemy, and restore our faith."

She felt a peace sweep over her. Her shivers ceased, and she opened her eyes. "You are a man after God, and I can see the love you have for Him." She put realization to his action. "Because I am His, He protects me, and I shouldn't fear anything. He'll show me the truth. I want to believe you. I want to know we're all going to be safe. It's difficult for me to trust you. I feel like I don't have time do that right now. Either I take the risk, or I don't, and we abandon hope and abandon what God is leading us to do."

"I'll give you space." He climbed halfway down the ladder. "But until then, I promise to do my best to protect each of you and this calling. I will not turn against you. I can't because I love you." He climbed down the rest of the way.

Essa kneaded her shoulder muscles and released some of the tension that had built up. She gazed over the small crested waves and concentrated on the sound of the water lapping against the sides of the vessel. A bug flew around her head, and she instinctively swatted at it. It flew across her vision, close enough to see yellow and black stripes. She squealed and ran to the ladder as fast as she could to avoid getting stung.

"In a hurry?" Amana asked.

"A bee!" Essa pointed out of breath and chuckled at her fear of a tiny insect.

"We are miles away from shore," Camille said. "It's too far for a bee. It was probably a gnat."

"No, no. A honey bee," Essa demanded.

Amana scrambled up to the captain's wheel and looked all around. A buzzing sound zoomed behind her. It was a honey bee. "Grandma Mile," she murmured. She shouted to the others, "It's time! Get your dive gear on."

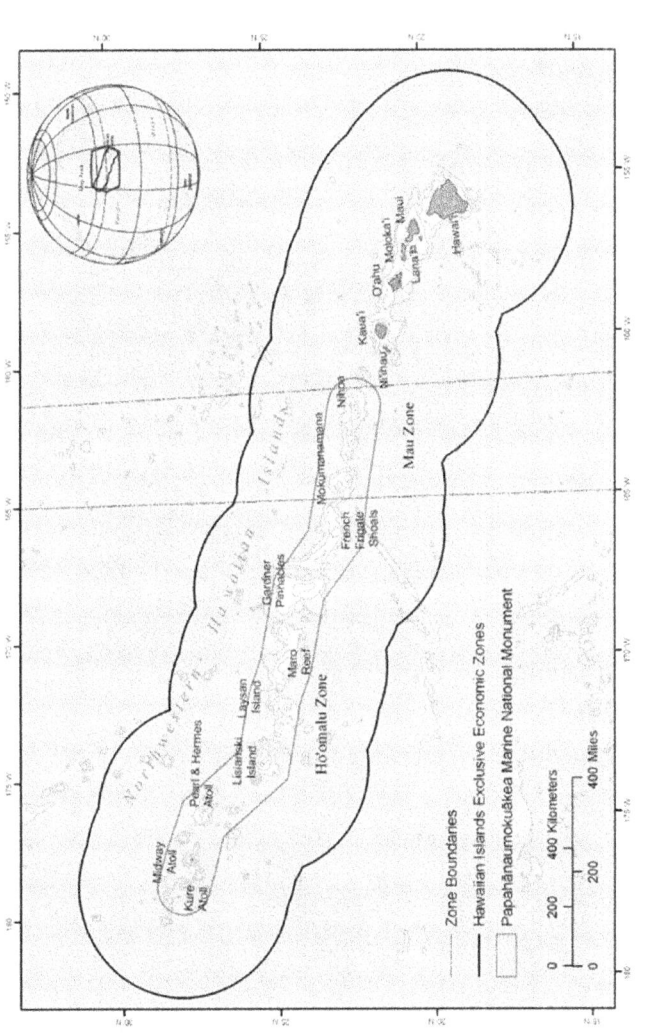

Chapter 19

Amana swung the wheel of the boat sharply to the right. It lifted the vessel's side and sliced an arc in the air. "Listen up!" she yelled below. "I'm going to drop Essa and Camille close to the site."

"Amana, wait till Bockman is in view. Coast in the opposite direction and drop me off. I'm hoping he'll follow me. That way I can keep you girls safe," Ryland instructed her.

"Ok," Camille added, "pretend you are on the trail to something. Act as if you have an agenda and are headed to a specific place."

Ryland grabbed the hose from a regulator. "I'll go southeast along the current."

Amana checked the coordinates on the global positioning system, ensured she was close to the underwater maze and volcanic vents, and put the boat in neutral. The motor toned down to a humming pulse. "This is it, ladies."

Essa squeezed her arm into her pink and black neoprene suit and motioned for her sister to jump in first. She tried pushing the lever to turn on her flashlight, and after several attempts it lit.

Camille hobbled with her fins to the deck. She secured her

mask and regulator on her face, got into a kneeling position, and let her body fall into the water on her back. A splash of water shot in the air. Her head surfaced.

Essa took that as her cue to join her. She plopped in and took her sister's hand. They raised their buoyancy control deflator hoses and gently descended.

The red glow stick pulsed on the back of her sister's tank. Her eyes followed the beam from their flashlights. The sandy bottom came into view, and they tapped the valve button to inflate a little air into their vests. They glided a few feet off the sand and shined their lights ahead.

Camille tugged on Essa's hand. Essa looked down at the compass. She extended her arm to show Camille and pointed ahead.

A blue ball of light jetted from the side and swam past the two girls. Essa recognized the deep sea angler. Flecks of gold shimmered below her just as before, leading a curved path to their left. She kicked her fins and propelled after the fish instead. *I refuse to follow the temptation of riches*, she reflected. Camille swam after her, trailing a mere ten feet behind.

As Essa got closer to the fish, she was able to tell it was roughly the same size as the one she and Ryland saw earlier. She had to wonder whether God was trying to show them that, yes, this was the way.

Camille checked her depth gauge. It read eighty-seven feet. She had forgotten to ask just how far down this 'tree' was. She recalled Essa only had a recreational diver's certification and could not descend past one hundred and thirty feet.

The angler fish stopped. Essa shined her flashlight at the massive stone structure. She kneeled on the bottom and wrote on her white slate.

Camille came up behind her and read her writing, *We are at the gate. Now we need to find the pearl.*

Camille scoured the crevices between the boulders and

caressed the smooth surface. She felt side to side, scanning the blockade.

She remembered what Essa had told her about the cross necklace she wore underneath her wetsuit. Camille felt a bit of doubt, despite the research, that simply thinking of something could change the chemistry in a person's brain. That was Satan, and she knew better than to believe that. She closed her eyes and focused on the cross and its meaning. Peace passed over her soul, and she relaxed.

Camille reopened them and reached out in front of her. She felt a rounded surface nestled snug in the crack of one large stone. She shined her light into the tiny passage, and an opal-colored gleam radiated from an object the size of a silver dollar. She took her metal rod and tapped it against her tank, creating a loud ting.

Essa appeared out of the dark, shined her light on it, and nodded to Camille. Essa wrote out a prayer on the board. *Where there are two or more in prayer, He is there.*

They took each other's gloved hand. Camille silently prayed, "*Heavenly Father, lift the cloud from our eyes so we may see the way to You. Amen.*"

They dropped hands and scanned the stronghold. Essa swam along the wall with her shoulder against it. She slipped and landed on another wall two feet in. She looked ahead and saw a path. She didn't realize there was a break by looking at the wall head-on, but feeling along it proved it had formed an L shape.

She stuck her head out of the opening and shined her light. Camille swam to her and entered the passageway. They mazed around the walls and felt a consuming heat. Essa cautioned her to move slowly. They swam around the next wall. Expansive, ten foot tall flames formed a circle. They were so thick that Camille could not see what lay beyond.

Flickering glows cast upon the wave-formed motions in the sand. The heat certainly commanded their respect. Its mighty force led Camille to question their safety.

She knew her loyalty to God was one that could withstand spiritual warfare and remembered that to the impure of heart, part of the ichthus would appear like one of the many ripples in the sand. Camille wrote on her board and showed it to Essa. *Look for the drawing of the ichthus.*

Essa nodded and placed her gaze downward.

Camille felt the strong urge to follow Essa. She hovered above her sister and waited.

A curved line caught Essa's peripheral vision. She quickly moved to the location and drew the other half of the ichthus, as in the story she had heard from Pastor Gill.

A blaze of fire subdued. Essa looked up at Camile, an elated look on her face. The gap through the fire was just enough space for a person to get through without suffering burns. Essa took Camille's clipboard and wrote *This is real!*

She glided over to the gap and could see that just beyond was the very top of a gigantic tree. Floating green leaves swayed in the drifts. It appeared as it would if it were on land. She looked down from the crown of the canopy. The distance looked to be fifty feet to where the large trunk settled into the ocean floor. She motioned for Camille to follow her on the descent.

They sank slowly and took in the sites around them. Balls of poofy yellow flowers dotted the branches. Scores of butterfly fish surrounded a few, picking at them with their tiny mouths. Bright red swollen seed pods coiled themselves near sets of twelve large thorns.

Camille landed on her knees and stabilized her body. Her eyes followed the massive trunk of sprouting branches. The leaves seemed like an umbrella offering protection. There is no way a tree could act as a portal. She waved for Essa's attention and pointed up.

Essa shook her head in confusion.

Camille wrote on her board *Eating the fruit altered Adam and Eve.*

They were altered due to their act of sin, not what they ate, Essa wrote back.

I feel that's a part of the strategy. It's worth a try.

Adam and Eve ate from the tree of knowledge not the tree of life. Essa marked.

Camille nodded her approval. She took a moment to write something on her board and then propelled herself upward with her arms and kicked her flippers to reach a curled pod. She popped it open and extracted a seed. She took her regulator out of her mouth and bit the juicy fruit.

Their clipboards drifted like feathers to the ocean bottom.

Chapter 20

Ryland climbed the ladder to the pilot house and sat in the chair next to Amana.

Her cell phone rang, and she fumbled to answer it.

Panic rang in Stern's voice. "I tried Essa's phone but she didn't answer. Where are you? And why does the sound have so much static?"

"We're off the coast of Pearl and Hermes Reef, just barely close enough to Midway to get a connection. We're headed to Lisianski Island. Essa and Camille just dove, why?"

"I got word Bockman is headed toward you. You've gotta get out of there! They won't let anyone get in the way of what they're after."

"They?"

"He has a group with him, including Hugh."

Amana and Hugh had worked together on many occasions, and she had trusted him. All this time he was Bockman's cohort. She grew numb.

Ryland snapped his fingers in front of her face to get her attention. She shook the feeling and regained control.

Light between the Leaves

"How do you know?" she asked Sterns.

"He phoned me to locate the deed to the land. He said he'd have the details wrapped up shortly. When I asked where he was, he said on a boat near Midway." His pitch elevated, whether from worry about her safety or his own future, she didn't know.

"Radio the Coast Guard," she told him, "and I'll do my best to keep them at bay." She ended the call.

Amana had approximately thirty minutes to come back to the site and search for the girls. They had just enough air for an hour-long dive.

"Ryland, Bockman is coming after us. I'm going head south to try to throw them off." She took a deep breath. "After you dive off the boat, I want you to wait approximately ten minutes, then resurface."

"What's that going to accomplish?"

"It will buy us time until the Coast Guard can find us."

Ryland looked skeptical about her plan. "Do you realize we are three hours from them at best?"

"Not if they have a station on Midway." She dismissed his rationality and continued, "I want to make them think you are headed to the Tree and hope they will drop a diver to follow you. Once they go down and you resurface, climb back in the boat. We'll drive out to the girls and pick them up."

"You do know that this man is deranged, right? We're putting our lives at risk for a tree we don't know is even there."

"We're already in this mess. Pray hard."

Amana jetted southeast. She could see a cabin cruiser in the distance. That must be them, she thought and pushed the throttle at full speed.

Ryland glanced in the rearview mirror. The vessel was gaining on them.

"I'm gonna have to drop you soon."

"That's fine. I won't be too far away from the girls then."

She pulled the throttle into neutral and waited until the cruiser got close enough for someone to see Ryland dive. They motored twenty-five feet from her hull. She could see Bockman standing at the bow of his boat.

Bockman raised a megaphone to his mouth. "Let us board. We have something you need."

Deception will never get you anywhere, Amana thought. There is no way I'm letting them on.

"We have your friend."

Amana turned and saw a girl struggling in Bockman's arms. His hand covered her mouth, and she had a cloth bag over her head. Amana couldn't tell whether it was Essa or Camille. She stopped her engines.

"We will give her back unharmed if you tell us where the Tree is. That is all we want."

How could she risk her friends' lives? She couldn't leave the girls there. She had to let Bockman board and give up their findings. Nothing was as precious as life.

"Come down from the cabin and stand at the back of your boat," he instructed.

She complied. The cruiser pulled up close enough for Hugh to grab the back of Amana's boat. Bockman released the girl. She pulled off the bag and started to laugh. It wasn't Essa or Camille. Bockman had lied.

Hugh jumped over the side of the craft and onto the dive platform. Amana tried to run toward the ladder to get to the wheel. Hugh caught her ankle. She tripped and hit her face on the bench. Her lip busted open, and her vision blurred.

Ryland submersed and floated twenty feet from the surface. The engine of the other boat rumbled closer. Amana would never let them board. She would take off before that could happen. What was going on? He looked upward and saw the other water craft cut the engines and drift toward theirs. Something's wrong. He needed to find the girls and warn them. The Coast Guard had been called. Maybe that would give them a little more time to get to Essa and Camille before the developers did.

Light between the Leaves

He descended, feeling the strong pull of the current. It would take him close to where the girls had been dropped off. He shined his flashlight on his compass and headed in the correct direction. The angler came from the side and swooshed ahead. Ryland followed it, not quite sure why but feeling that he should.

In a few moments, Ryland arrived at the gate. He prayed once again and drew the ichthus in the sand. The red fire subsided, and he entered.

The sight of the Tree was the same as in his dream. The veins through each-three foot leaf flowed as if they were in a rushing stream. He traced his gloved hands along the rough bark. Its scabrous trunk snagged the fabric.

He floated down to the sandy bottom and saw a clipboard. He glanced around. Essa and Camille were nowhere to be found. He picked up the board and read it. They had deciphered the clues and left instructions for him. Eat one seed from a pod, and then a whole flower, and finally a fruit. Wait ten minutes for the reaction. It worked if we are not here.

How would a small chemical reaction like that make their whole bodies disappear? He knew this was not a magic act. After all, don't people with near death stories *return* to their bodies?

He cupped his hands, held his arms to his sides, and propelled himself up the side of the tree to get a better look. Ryland saw thin, bright yellow stripes on a figure lying on the other side of the trunk. He dove downward, heart pounding. He knew better than to hyperventilate because it would use up his air supply quicker, but he didn't care. His eyes were able to distinguish two figures. Essa was lying on her back, still clenching the regulator between her teeth. Her eyes were closed. He rolled up a sleeve of her wetsuit and checked her pulse. It was faint.

He dropped her wrist and examined her supply of air. It was enough to last her nearly an hour! After being down as long as she had, she should've run out by now. He feared that she had stopped breathing. He tore his glove off and placed his hand on her chest, monitoring the regulator to detect respiration. It was very shallow but present.

It took him a few minutes to process the oddity of the situation. He flexed his ankles and used the force to get himself up to one of the coiled pods. He cracked one of the seed shells open. It revealed a luscious, bright-red sphere. He ate it and did the same with a pompon-like flower. He broke the fruit's skin with his teeth and dug into its tender sweetness.

Ryland watched the minutes go by. He felt light headed, and his eyes became heavy. He closed his lids and felt the water swirl around him. He opened them. A whirlpool twisted upward from the top of the tree. The leaves seemed undisturbed. It was roughly the width of the leafy umbrella. He prayed for guidance and remembered that something special happened when normal matter met with exotic matter.

His intentions were pure. He placed his index finger in the middle of the circular churning. His spirit left his body and elevated weightlessly into the vortex. A warm white light enveloped him. There was no sound. Time seemed to slow. His mind became alert and acutely aware of each stimulus. A tunnel appeared as a river, with distinct circular walls characteristic of transparent crystal.

This cannot be happening. I must be in a dream. The light faded, and his spirit body began to fall.

Faith, faith, think of God's love, he repeated to himself. The light increased, and he continued his journey upward. A bright radiance shone from above. He touched a ray and experienced comforting heat throughout his body.

Any cares he had slipped away. His face glowed with the light. His mind was wrapped in an all-consuming love. The encounter transcribed to each body part; anything he touched, looked at, heard, tasted, or smelled increased his overall sense of being loved and the experience of sheer joy.

Then he felt what he could not describe, a sixth sense perhaps? A feeling of a growing need yet to be fulfilled. When he was

Light between the Leaves

practically on top of the bright light, he was expelled through a crystal river. His head surfaced. The water sparkled in opalescence with every color. Abundance of sea life in unimaginable hues cascaded through the waters.

The river flowed from a golden glowing throne and continued throughout the land. An auroral illumination penetrated from the chest of God. It revealed the polychromatic weave of space. Without his physical body, he was now witness to the realm of multi-dimensions. He was interacting with every *part* of every*thing*.

Each substance, the river, God's throne, the brilliant gold pathways, and greenish landscapes, were revealed as sequenced patterns. Twelve trees bearing twelve crops of fruit lined each side of the river. A few leaves dropped and drifted along the current and disappeared into a tiny whirlpool.

He wanted to laugh and cry with happiness, but no sound came out of his mouth. A magnificently tall being approached him and spoke without words, spirit to spirit, though his mind interpreted her thoughts as words. She was revealing her curiosity and cheerful spirit.

Past the trees, he saw twelve gates made of pearl. He wanted to climb onto the bank of the river toward one of the gates. His soul drifted towards them, obeying his thoughts. He got closer to the trees. Their cube-like dimensions allowed him to see between the colorful impressed lines. He realized that he could mesh with this life, for life it was, as was everything he experienced.

Ryland stretched his hand and penetrated a leaf. He felt the vibration of nutrients flowing through it. He pulled his arm back.

Animals and people bustled about. They played and sang praises toward the radiance. People from different cultures and races were farming together. The only way to describe their appearance was according to their former physical beings, but they consisted more of an energy mass. Each of them had specific characteristics, yet each was surrounded in a phosphorescent glimmer. There was no weakness to hold them back from accomplishing anything good.

A woman raised herself up from worship and turned around. It was Essa. She ran into his arms and embraced him. They melded together, and he could feel a freedom of pain, fear, sadness, guilt, jealousy and anxiety. What remained was a pure happiness unlike he had ever known—a simple, warm comfort. He could not only see her joy but also feel it. He experienced it throughout his being.

She was eager to introduce him to people. Two woman coated in brilliant reds and oranges drifted over. He recognized one as Camille. She motioned to the other woman. "This is my sister, Corinne," she said.

He received her sister's personality. She was curious, a trusting soul untouched by years of pain. Pure. She shot off bursts of energy, the result of her enthusiasm for their presence.

"We can see Him now." Essa took his hand. She led him across a prism over to the throne, bowed down, and sang in a beautiful voice. It wasn't so much a melody as it was an adoration transcribed into musical notes.

God's body of light gave off a cadence of vibrations and created a blend of colors in a circle encompassing his throne with shades of jasper and carnelian. Waves of warmth from his image emanated from him. A throng of elders held golden bowls on each side of the throne. Each bowl had the word "prayer" etched on the front. They reached in and threw a handful of thin, shimmering silver into the air that drifted in front of God. He blew His breath on them, and the prayers were answered.

Ryland had retained a small portion of his connection to bodily life, and the Lord's intense frequency was almost too much to handle. God's essence affected him strongly, yet he felt a gentle touch from His light, soothing their questions. Ryland desired to be captivated in Him forever.

God transferred loving ambiance into their spirits and explained how they had the ability to transcend their bodies into heaven with His allowance. "Faith and obedience has gotten you here. You each overcame your doubt, so I gave you the right to eat from the Tree of Life in my paradise."

God opened the palm of his hand, revealing seven points of light. Each one grew larger until it took on a shape they recognized as angels. They were different in appearance from the other souls. The light they emanated was wispy and flickering. The souls they had seen were dense and consistent. The angels appeared airy, and they did not seem to offer their own thoughts but carried out God's command.

"All angels are ministering spirits sent to serve those who will inherit salvation," God clarified. "The people and animals are one in spirit and purpose. They are helping me to prepare the new heaven on earth. I've allowed a few people to enter heaven, such as yourselves, in order to return and let others know they may receive forgiveness of their sins and have a place with me sanctified by faith. You are to guide people to an earthly resurgence of the Christian faith."

"I have essential wisdom for you to relay. Tell Amana I have appointed her as guardian to protect the wildlife of the northwestern islands and to carry on what her grandfather started. She is to show people the significance of my creations and allow their respect to grow from that experience. Remind her of her courage. She feels she is not strong, yet I dwell in her and will make her so."

"Can you help us defeat Bockman and the others?" Ryland begged. "I'm afraid I cannot resist him on my own."

God sent a warming sensation to Ryland. "Regarding your opposition, speak over your enemies with scripture and prayers for healing. As I've had the prophets write in My book, I say, at the present time, your plenty will supply what they need, so that in turn their plenty will supply what you need. Then there will be equality."

Camille looked around her. "I don't want to leave. Please let me stay."

"I will return you all to your earthly dwelling, but you will have an intense longing to come back to me. Do not act on this, as I will be the one to let you know when your job is complete. Teach others, share the gifts I've given you, and learn in preparation for helping me build heaven on earth. I will allow you to receive joy in reuniting with your family. Then you must go back. One of my dwelling places is earth. We are still connected in every mansion I have created. It does not matter which one you are in because I am there."

"Are there levels of heaven, Lord?" Essa asked.

"Each of you is loved equally and bought with the same price."

They knelt at God's feet. He lifted them, enveloped in his strong, comforting arms. Essa didn't want to ever leave her Heavenly Father. God felt her emotion and spoke once more. "I will give you a special gift, a partnership to last a lifetime. You and Ryland will be joined and will shelter one another with agape love."

She smiled and knew forgiveness must be in her heart for him. Her wrongs were open for others to see, and she hoped Ryland would forgive her misdoings. Essa poured out her guilt of judging others, especially her sister, Camille, and the weakness of her spirit in faith. She had turned from those who needed uplifting. A wave of joy swept over her spirit and washed away the shame. She was healed and could go forth on a smooth path.

An older gentleman approached her, offering his hand. She placed hers in his with question. His laugh was sincere. "I'm Noah, Amana's grand-daddy." His voice was deep and silky. He led her along the path. She understood what he was saying as the Holy Spirit translated his thoughts into words. Essa had to concentrate on his words. There was so much to witness in heaven.

"I thought when people passed away, their bodies become the age of Jesus when he died."

"This body?" he said grinning. "This vision of a body is

for you. Otherwise, it might be difficult for you to trust." He looked down at himself and said, "Let me show you the new and improved me."

He let go of her hand, lifted his head in praise, and allowed the light to penetrate his chest. Bursts of soft glowing rays shot from his heart and slowly took over the rest of his body. He was in no particular shape but was instead a mass of glimmering energy. His thoughts and speech were transformed into vibrations. "I will receive an even more glorious figure once Jesus returns to earth and joins our soul and physical body together." Slowly he faded back into his earthly form.

They exited the golden brick path and climbed a grassy hill. It overlooked the river, forests, the throne of God being the largest, most radiant sight.

Noah broke the silence. "The Lord made Amana to carry out his plans of planet restoration. She is his ambassador and continues what I began. It will soon be time for her to take her position in political leadership to guide others."

"Does she know this?"

"In her heart, she does, but earthly concerns and anxiety easily mask that. You need to remind her. Will you do that?"

"Of course."

"Help her on the front lines and teach the others. Harvest the leaves from the Tree of Life each month for healing."

She understood him to mean that she should bring more people to Christ.

"I have a request. Tell my granddaughter that on her acacia bracelet, I had etched a small word that the Lord told me so I would remember to keep on course."

"Did you make that bracelet for your wife from the thorns of the Tree?"

"Yes," he confirmed. "Also, tell Meli to look behind the dresser. She lost a love letter I had mailed her when I was in the service."

"I'll do that, but she may think I'm crazy."

"Not at all. It will calm her concerns and let her know I'm thinking of them all."

Essa's spirit contemplated how she could make things right on earth.

Noah took Essa's hand and smiled. "Yes," he replied to thin air, and then prayed, "Lord, please open her eyes so she can see her messenger."

Her eyes involuntarily closed. When she reopened them, a congregation of spirits appeared to take up space as far as her vision allowed. There were so many types of angels. Some were tall with six wings, while others were opaque objects. She was overwhelmed by their waves of feelings, adoration, glory, and thankfulness, all directed toward the Light.

She collapsed. Noah caught her. She breathlessly whispered. "Angels?" He grinned. She steadied on her feet. "How did I not see them before?"

One drifted up beyond the horizon and floated toward her. His gleaming bronze feet were framed behind two of his twelve wings. Eyes dotted the feathers and blinked at her. He wore white clothing, but his body glowed a soft green. He had a gold belt that came into view as he lowered. His top two wings covered his head. They slowly opened, revealing four faces. One looked like a man, the other reflected the face of Christ, the third a servant, and on the far right, an eagle.

Essa was struck with awe. Electric pulses shot from his body in a magnificent movement. His voice reverberated as he spoke. "You wonder." He pointed to the glass floor underneath them. A circle slowly opened. She could see several of his beings. They flung swords into a chaos of dark souls.

"He commands me to guard you, and I will lift you in my hands. You will tread upon the serpent and trample him."

"Why?" She could not help but ask. The word tumbled out of her thoughts.

"He loves you. He will protect and rescue you because you know Him. You are to call on God, and He'll answer you."

Light between the Leaves

"What is *that*?" She pointed a shaky finger to the circle of fighting below her.

"War. These are God's angels and the wicked fallen ones in battle on earth as we speak. Being in a body limits your sight. He will use those evil ones to carry out His purpose toward a final defeat, asserting His judgment and taking His rightful place."

She could see people among the angels. "They don't know you are there, do they?"

He shook his heads.

The souls of the people of God were illuminated brightly. They produced loving feelings. She also saw spirits that were dark and empty, yet each one of them had a faint orange flicker. One of those beings cried and shouted out to God. The orange swelled. A beam shot past her to the soul. She looked around and saw that it came from the throne. God was sharing His light and sending it directly the man. She turned her head back to the circle. The man calmed, and they could hear him speak over the noise of the continuous battle.

"Save me! You are real, God, and I am yours." His orange glow took over his entire body, from the tips of his fingers to the toes on his feet. God had proliferated this phenomenon.

A throng of angels in heaven rejoiced and sang. Noah and the angel joined.

Essa nodded. "I want to be His warrior."

Ryland lifted his head from the ground before God's feet. He heard a series of sharp barks and a panting noise. The noise came closer. A slobbery tongue licked the back of his head. He turned around and saw his labrador, Petra, who had passed away when he was in his teens. Her brown and gray coat was shiny and soft. She used to be mangy from burs in the woods.

Petra held her chest out with pride and trotted.

He opened his arms and tightly hugged her. Tears of happiness flooded his eyes. They lifted from his eyes and floated away in tear shaped bubbles.

She leapt in circles around him when he let go.

He turned to God. "I wasn't sure animals made it to heaven."

"They, just like you, have the ability to embrace the light or choose darkness. I have created each creature and plant to fulfill a purpose. Yours is different from that of an animal, yet you each have your role on earth and in heaven."

Ryland's smile grew, and he ran toward the field with Petra chasing after him.

Camille sang to the Lord in a triumphant, strong voice. She rarely allowed herself to sing so strongly on earth. Here, her confidence soared. A girl with shagged, chin-length hair kneeled beside her. Camille jumped at feeling her presence. She recognized the soul next to her. Could it be? Camille opened her eyes and shook her head. "Corinne!" She grabbed her twin sister and squeezed. "I'm sorry that it was you who didn't make it and not me." She pulled back to look at her.

Corinne's nose was short and upturned, with a spray of freckles. Her dainty figure was wrapped in a radiant, flowing, light-pink dress.

"It was the other way around, Camille. I have never had to feel pain or suffering, never had to learn what a lost love felt like." She smiled. "Look at me!" She stood up and twirled in a circle. Her glorious body glistened with beauty. "I have been spared. Come, let me show you what my life has been since we last saw each other. This will also be your home someday." Corinne raised one arm in the air.

"What are you doing?" Camille asked.

"Isn't this what you do on earth so a superhero can fly?"

Camille stared at her a moment, then burst into laughter. "You are trying to put things into my perspective." She raised her arms as well, and they lifted high above heaven. The smell of flower blossoms came from all directions. They crested mountains, dipped into valleys, and landed on the plains to play with the wild animals. There was no aggression.

"The fight over food or a mate isn't needed in heaven. The lamb can cuddle with the lion and be happy." She saw an alligator basking on the river bank and kissed its snout. She looked intently at her sister. "Camille, you have to stop living for me. We are two very different souls."

"I *have* been doing that."

"Spend your time investing in relationships that last. Your feelings will get hurt, but that is a part of sin and forgiveness. You will forgive and move on in your relationships with strength that wasn't there before."

Camille embraced her sister. "Spending this time with you has been so precious. It has opened my eyes and freed my future."

Camille frowned. "I can't hear your voice once I get back on earth. I will miss this."

"The Lord allows you to feel my words directed to you. It will be but a second, and then we'll be joined again."

"It won't feel like that to me."

"Look for signs. I'll be saying hello to you when you see pink lady slipper posies. Listen and allow God to work in your life, and you will feel my love shining through."

Chapter 21

Ryland, Essa, and Camille each felt a tug on their hearts. God was ready to release them back to earth. They met and walked to the spot they had come through in the river. The only way Essa was able to rationalize leaving was that she knew without a doubt that she would be back.

The white horizon opened up, and the warm waters swirled. The vacuum became stronger and shifted them downward. Essa felt as if she were standing still while everything else around her moved. She was told to focus on her body and earth. They shot through the ocean, and once they come past the top of the Tree of Life, everything slowed, and they drifted down. Essa could see their bodies lying on the sand at the base of the Tree. In an instant, they were thrust into their bodies. She was able to feel her muscles moving and air flowing in her lungs. She took a moment to adjust to being back in her body.

She checked her gauges and assessed how much air remained. Camille and Ryland were doing the same. Camille pointed to her air level. Essa glanced over and saw it was low. She held her finger up as a sign for them to start their ascension back to the surface.

Light between the Leaves

She had no idea how much time had lapsed but her thoughts quickly turned to Amana.

Essa spotted bubbles rising from below. She patted Ryland's arm. Two men in dive suits ascended at a quickened pace from the sea floor.

Ryland could read the words "Planet Care" on their wetsuits and relaxed. He remembered Amana had called for the Coast Guard hours ago and expected they had alerted the eco-tour company to assist. The divers motioned for Camille, Essa, and Ryland to follow them. They rose to fifteen feet and all hovered in the water for three minutes. Essa helped Camille remain calm, and had her take shallow, spaced-out breaths.

They broke the surface and the eco tour divers signaled to a far away boat. The waves were high, but Camille spit the regulator out of her mouth and breathed deeply.

"Are you all right?" Ryland asked her.

She nodded and turned to one of the eco divers. "How were you able to find us? Did you get Bockman and his men?"

They kept their regulators in their mouths and did not reply. One of the guys nodded.

The boat circled the divers and cut the motor. Two other men stood at the back, pulled each one up and helped them to their seats. Ryland slipped off his gear and helped the others. A large shadow cast behind him. He turned around to see Bockman, face to face.

"Thanks for bringing us our little treasures." He patted him on the back. "Only a few more things to wrap up, and you will have that position."

Ryland decided to play along. "Sure thing, boss. So where are we headed?" Something out of the corner of Ryland's eye caught his attention. Essa screamed. Hugh Kiebert's body was slumped against the wall.

"Hugh decided he was better than all of us and didn't want to make waves," Bockman explained with an evil laugh. "I wanted to save my bullets just in case, so I drugged him instead." He checked his watch. "We won't have to worry about him for another four hours or so. As for you ladies, I'll need to get a bit of information." He took out his pistol from his shorts and gestured with it in the air.

"And then what?" Camille said, seething. "What are you going to do if we don't?"

Essa punched Ryland on the shoulder. "You promised me!" Essa shouted at him.

"Promises are broken every day" Bockman replied. "Boys, until these ladies decide they're going to cooperate, restrain them below."

The two fake eco divers and two other men grabbed Camille and Essa. They wrestled with them and secured zip ties around their wrists and ankles. They picked them up, pulled them down a few steps, and threw them on hard benches.

Ryland devised a plan. He knew the bathroom was attached to the room the girls were in.

"Where are you headed?" Bockman asked Ryland.

"Urinal." No one was the wiser. He saluted and made his way to the front of the boat. He unlocked the door. The girls were lying on the benches. He shut the door quietly behind him.

He approached them and motioned to keep quiet, opening the ties that held them. "I'm going to release you," he whispered. "There's a dinghy on the side of the boat that has enough gas to get you back to Midway. I think they took Amana there. Remember, in Ephesians, God says to put on His full armor so that you can take your stand against the devil's schemes."

One of Bockman's henchman stepped into the room. Ryland pushed the guy into the bathroom and stuck a pin in the door, locking him inside. Two more men came in response to the chaos, and the girls kicked and pushed them toward the benches, giving themselves space to flee toward the dinghy. They saw Bockman on the upper deck with the captain.

They climbed into the dingy, and Ryland lowered them into the water. He pulled the cord to start the engine.

Light between the Leaves

Bockman heard the commotion. He ran towards the railing, grabbing a paddle from the side of the boat. Camille held the handle on the motor and steered them toward Midway Atoll. Essa looked back.

Bockman struck the back of Ryland's head with the wide end of the paddle. Ryland turned around and was hit again near his hairline. A rush of blood spouted and trailed down his face.

Essa screamed, "No!" She sobbed and placed her hands together and channeled her helplessness into God's protection. "Dear Lord, help Ryland take Your helmet of salvation, protect him from any more harm, and give him the sword of Your word!" She watched the scene grow farther and farther away.

Chapter 22

Amana's lashes fluttered, and she realized she was coming to. Her lips pulsed in pain, and her head ached. She licked a sticky substance on her mouth. It was dried blood. She was bruised, hungry, and thirsty. An itchy rope tied her arms to the back of the chair where she was bound.

The room was damp and dark. There didn't appear to be anyone with her. She kept still and listened but only heard her own breathing. The knots were too tight to offer any chance of escape. She lifted her butt off the chair barely an inch and twisted herself to the side. With some difficulty and a little pain, she managed to finagle her arms around the chair's spindles and off the backing. Whoever put me here, she thought, was never a boy scout.

Amana could not fathom how large a place she was in or whether there was a door. If there were a door, someone might be waiting outside it. She decided to take her chances. Her arms were still tied. She walked backwards in an attempt to run into a wall. It took about twenty steps until she contacted a cold metal wall. Where on earth was she?

Light between the Leaves

Facing away from the wall, she ran her fingers along the surface, seeking a door, an opening, anything that might help her escape. Her fingers found a rather deep crevice. She jumped up to feel for a latch or handle. She leapt up again. Her hands felt a long lever, and she grabbed hold.

She stood on her toes and reached up as far as she could, but it pulled her forearm muscles farther than they wanted to go. She moaned in pain. Her hair stuck to her sweating cheeks. She tried once more. The lever gave a sharp squeak. The door flew open, and she dropped to the ground. She rolled to her side, threw herself onto her knees, and stood up.

A crack of dawn's light blasted through the door, burning her eyes. Ok, she was outside. Short trees and bushes scattered over the terrain. Waves were crashing somewhere off to her side.

A dilapidated, rectangular building stood close by. She ran and hid behind it.

Essa and Camille rammed the dinghy onto the sand and ran into the dense forest of Midway Atoll.

"I know this is a small island, but I have no idea where we're going," Essa said, panting.

"Neither do I, but its size can work to our advantage. We're bound to run into something soon."

They dodged branches and headed for cover among the shoulder-high weeds. To their right, they heard men talking. They crouched hiding in the overgrowth. One of the two men was the owner of the dive boat they had rented. It looked like one of Bockman's men was turning in their rented water craft.

"That must have been the man who took Amana," Camille whispered. "She has got to be here!"

"All we have to do now is find her and fight off Bockman's thugs, but with what, I don't know."

"What are you worried about? God always wins. Let's pray a prayer of protection over us and Amana."

They bowed their heads and spoke to the Lord. The girls

came across the vestige of a WWII bunker with its door half open. Essa motioned to Camille. They ran to building and looked in. The light illuminated the inside enough to see a wooden chair tipped on its side.

"That must have been for Amana. Do you think she escaped?" Essa asked.

"I don't know." Footsteps crunched around the side of the building, coming closer. "We'd better head back for cover." Camille ran for the safety of the brush, and Essa trailed closely behind.

They watched as the man saw the open door and quickened his pace. He looked in the building and pounded his fist on the metal wall. He turned in a half circle, feverishly looking for his captive, but she was nowhere in sight. He cursed several times.

The girls played cat and mouse with the man. They scurried to the back of a long structure. Amana stood with her hands behind her back.

"Amana!" Essa cried in a whisper. She wrapped her arms around her. Essa stepped back and surveyed her friend's condition. "No worries. We'll get you cleaned up."

"Please untie me! My arms burn," Amana begged.

Essa used her fingernails to untie the knots. Amana stretched her arms with a sigh.

"We have to keep moving. That man is searching for you!" Camille reminded them.

A large hand came from around the corner and grabbed Camille.

Bockman fastened her arms. She fought him in a desperate attempt to wiggle free.

He pulled a gun from the back of his pants and put it up to her temple. "No one is going anywhere."

Essa and Amana froze. Essa prayed to her Savior. A strange sound echoed in the air. Bockman looked up and around to see helicopters closing in on the island.

"Get into the bunker!" he yelled at them. They complied immediately. He threw Camille in with the other two and slid the lever back over the door. They heard him wedge something under the entrance. Essa tried to open it. Stuck, but maybe with just enough give she could knock loose whatever he had used.

She heard the helicopter land, and then someone shouted about following Bockman into the woods. The girls started pounding on the door and yelling for help. In moments, the door opened, and a Coast Guard officer looked inside. Hot tears ran down Essa's face. The officer got out a first aid kit from his back pack and attended to Amana.

The next helicopter landed near them. Winds whipped in circles, churning the dirt into swarms of dust. Essa could see Ryland, Bockman, and Hugh being led to the chopper, handcuffed.

A Coast Guard boat jetted up to the lone dock. A crowd of officers were poised in the front. As soon as the dock was reached, the police leapt off to meet up with the chopper crew. One motioned to the prisoners, and then another pointed to the boat.

Essa and Ryland met each other's gaze, and Essa ran to the chopper.

"You're all right!" he shouted over the sound of the chopper blades, his voice breaking with relief.

She reached out for him and kissed the gash on his forehead.

"Bockman . . . Well, he didn't like it when I released his prisoners . . . or that I was on God's side." He tried to stand in the chopper, as if he were about to jump out.

The guard beside Ryland grabbed him by his cuffs. "You're not escaping. Don't even think about it. It's the station for you, and then on to prison."

"Wait!" Essa screamed. "He's not one of them." The guard faced her. "Hugh Kiebert is innocent, too. Bockman admitted to drugging him once he discovered Hugh wasn't going to go along with his plan."

"Is this true?" he asked Amana and Camille. They nodded

and retold the story. The guard shrugged and pulled out his handcuff keys to release Ryland.

Ryland reached for Essa and pressed her small frame against his chest. She let his love soak into her fragile form.

Chapter 23

The Coast Guard took Hugh and Amana in one helicopter to the hospital on Oahu. Ryland refused to leave Essa. One of the guards applied a disinfectant, gave him pain medication, and painted on a liquid band aid. He instructed Ryland to head to the medical center when they landed. The other chopper held Bockman and flew off to the coast guard station for holding.

The final aircraft contained Essa, Ryland, and Camille. Essa sat realizing the gravity of the situation they endured. They had *more* than endured. They had *overcome*, thanks to their Savior. She would never think of God the same way again.

It was true; she desired with all her heart to be back in heaven and never have to deal with evil, physical trauma, or emotional suffering. But she had a job that involved thousands of lives. God entrusted her with a plan that she was determined to see through.

She had never realized the extent of God's love for her and others. It was beyond words, beyond this world. He trusted her to help sustain the ecology in preparation of heaven on earth and to show others the love He has for them. If only other people knew prayer wasn't about granting wishes of what new things they coveted. It was to gain a never-ending communion with their Heavenly Father who would take away pain, replacing it with immense joy! What amazing gifts He gave every single person. Each of them had a wild adventure to fulfill.

Essa glanced at Ryland sitting next to her. The blood from his injury had left a dried trail down the side of his temple. She wrapped her arms around him and leaned on his shoulder. They had so much going for them. If they could get through what they just endured, they could make it through anything.

Camille caught her eye, and Essa wondered how she'd decide to live out her life now that she was released from guilt. Would everything change or would she expect to hear from her sister once in a blue moon? She was suddenly filled with dread.

The chopper landed on the launch pad at the Coast Guard facility. An ambulance was waiting for Ryland. Essa rode with him to the hospital. Doctors scanned his head for any fractures and determined there were none. He received stitches on his wounds and a bottle of antibiotics to take home.

Essa went to check on Amana. She knocked on her hospital room door and heard women talking. Amana's Aunt 'Akau and Grandma Meli sat on the edge of the bed. Amana appeared to be exhausted from the day's events. There were tiny red marks around her wrists.

"How are you feeling?" Essa asked and handed her a balloon she had gotten from the gift shop.

"Nervous. When Bockman and his men took over our boat, they drugged me. I awoke in the dark bunker with my hands and feet tied."

Aunt 'Akau smoothed Amana's hair. "They took blood samples from her and Hugh to figure out what Bockman had given them. They're analyzing them now."

"They want to monitor her overnight," Grandma Meli added.

"Good idea," Essa said.

'Akau smiled. "Hugh may be acquitted from any charges. He gave the police his statements, and I've been reviewing them. According to Mr. Kiebert, Bockman had requested him to help with a project and told him they were going to do sport fishing."

"Fishing for us!" Essa practically shouted. "Where *is* Bockman?" Even saying his name made Essa quiver.

"They have him in custody at the jail. Apparently Hugh had jumped over to Amana's boat with the intent of escaping. That is when Bockman drugged both of them."

"I hope they don't release him."

"He'll face trial for kidnapping, stealing university research information, and intent to kill," 'Akau told her.

"I'm thankful Hugh tried to save me from that nasty devil of a man," Amana admitted.

Essa got an idea. "Do you feel up to walking around the corner?" she asked her friend.

"Yes. I'm pretty tired, though, so just a short walk."

Amana leaned on Essa's arm for support, and the two of them hobbled into Hugh's hospital room. His wife, Tasha, got up from a chair, and gave Amana a gentle hug. "You're ok! My husband told me everything. My heart hurt for all you went through."

"It's over now," Essa said and then addressed Hugh. "I thought you might need some cheering up, as well." She handed him a plastic fishing pole with a magnet on the end and a stuffed diver attached to it.

He chuckled and immediately grabbed his side. "My ribs are a little beat up. It hurts to laugh, but I couldn't help it."

"Realizing what I could've lost made me see just how much I love him." Tasha leaned over and kissed Hugh.

"We have been through a lot, but that's what has brought us back together." He grabbed her hand and squeezed.

Tasha looked back at him. "There is one more secret to reveal. I figured since we were here at the hospital, I'd see why I'd been feeling so odd." She paused for effect. She fought to hide back her smile. "We're going to have a baby!"

Amana squealed, and Essa hugged her gently.

"Our first one! Four marriages for me and no kids. We're both determined to stay together forever and can't wait to see what a combo of us is going to be like." He laughed and clutched his side again.

"How far along are you?" Essa asked.

"Eight weeks."

"It will be nice to see a little one running around Planet Care and learning about ecology. It's so important to teach them young," Amana said.

Hugh and Tasha glanced at one another. "I hope you won't be too disappointed, but I want to spend more time at home. I still need a job though." When Amana didn't say anything, he continued, "Would you mind switching titles with me? I'm sure I could get the board to approve it."

She didn't know what to say.

"You've all been through so much today. Let's not overwhelm her," Tasha said.

"How about we talk in the morning over some of the hospital's finest coffee blend?" Amana giggled.

An entire year had almost passed. Essa retrieved a pen and paper out of her desk drawer and wrote a letter to Grandma Rose in her journal. Her pastor mentioned that it might help her get through her grandmother's death.

> *Many great changes are certain for all of our futures. The Governor of Hawaii signed an agreement with Nevada to transfer Bockman to their prison. Amana took up her new title as CEO of Planet Care. She has started to fulfill the prophesy that Grandma Meli and God had spoken of and is continuing the ecological guardianship for the northwest islands.*
>
> *I had a hard time saying goodbye to Camille,*

but she sends me letters all the time and calls often. She moved back to our home town seven months ago and decided she wanted to stop living life for her sister. She seems excited to begin making her own.

Hugh and Tasha renewed their vows and last week celebrated the next journey in life—their baby boy.

I'm still teaching botany at the university, and Ryland is working as youth pastor at our church. I'm excited to say that last night he proposed. I'm thankful to be getting married to a great Christian man and chose your beautiful backyard to exchange our vows. It will be this fall surrounded by our family and friends.

Did I ever find my purpose in life? Yes. I found there are countless ways God uses His creations to transform people's lives for the better. I thank our Lord for His patience with mankind. He rejoices in seeing the good in us develop and cheers us on as we reach fruition.

My destiny was not to find the Tree of Life but to use the time I have on earth to learn through experiences of love and teach others what I have discovered. It's all about sharing to help one another find their communion with God. I'm so glad you're experiencing what I only got a glimpse of. Until the day I come back home to heaven,

Yours in Christ,

Essa

Coming soon!

Shane's Shenanigans

Oops!
I spilled my glass of giggles AGAIN!
The comedic adventures of life with kids are captured
in this journal of childhood truths and fantasy.
It's woven with an abundance of hysterical situations, sure to
unleash your silliness. Some of my favorite books were written
by the late great Shel Silverstein. If you enjoy his works, you
will love Shane's Shenanigans woven in a similar style.
Laughter is a kiss from Heaven, blessing
everyone with God's joy.

Visit mollygshane.com!

Don't miss any of Shane's mystery, romance, and humor!

Two families divided by lies and secrets come together in their race to find the truth.

Kelsey Dane is an extended family member of the Royals. Each one's personality is distant and cold, except for Princess Victoria. Kelsey is entrusted to find a suitor for the princess. Will the perfect man she finds pick fame and fortune with the royal blood line or someone more prohibiting?

The Rumors. Everyone from their country whispers tales of her ancestors, forbidden love.

The Legacy. If Kelsey can unravel the mystery, she might be able to bring her family together again after centuries of separation. The truth unleashed could ruin her relative's legacy and end the reigning kingdom. Will she finally have the family she so desperately desires?

- **ISBN-10:** 1440101930
- **ISBN-13:** 978-1440101939

Available wherever books are sold or visit mollygshane.com to place an order.

My Glass Heart Can't Be Broken

Molly G. Shane

Cedrine Linstor thought there was no surviving a lost love until it happened to her. Her father's stroke had taken him away forever. Her mother was forced to work extra hours with little time for her. The only ones she could turn to were her childhood friends, Greg and Isaiah.

Isaiah's disability was shortly recognized by his teacher. His parents made the difficult decision to send him to a boarding school hours away where there was a specialized instructor.

Greg Merisotti worked at the horse ranch where Cedrine and Isaiah kept their mares, until a seminary graduate asked Greg to watch over his church. Greg had an epiphany there, which he shared with the young priest. The priest requested he attend a mission and look for God's signs to help figure out his future.

Cedrine had no one until she began receiving anonymous love letters. At first, it gave her hope, but as the letters kept coming, with each clue leading nowhere, she wanted to give up her search until she got an astounding idea. Will you be able to figure it out before Cedrine does? Let's find out!

- **ISBN-10:** 0595523692
- **ISBN-13:** 978-0595523696

Available wherever books are sold or visit mollygshane.com to place an order.

You know it's inside you, that kid you once knew. This book was written for that child in YOU! (young ones, too) So LAUGH! and let it all go... You can't fool me. I see that giggle. The child inside you wants to wiggle. Don't be afraid to let out a snicker. Be that as it may, my kids and I are the exact SAME way!!

Tu sabes que esta dentro de ti, ese niño que conociste algún día. Este libro fue escrito para ese niño ¡TU! (Y para los pequeños también.) Entonces ¡Ríete! y suelta todo... No me puedes engañar. Veo esa sonrisa. El niño dentro de ti quiere moverse. ¡¡No tengas miedo de dejar salir una risa disimulada!! Mis hijos y yo somos exactamente IGUAL!!

- **ISBN-10:** 9781440135262

- **ISBN-13:** 978-1440135262

Available wherever books are sold or visit mollygshane.com to place an order.

appendix

Fruits of the Spirit

Take pride in yourself. Your faith in Christ makes you worthy to enter the kingdom of God and receive eternal life!

Before we can begin to examine the *gifts* of the spirit, we need to look at the *fruits* of the spirit. Jesus puts the fruit above the gifts and asked us to master them. It is our goal as His followers to be proficient at EACH and possess ALL of these fruits according to **Galatians, Chapter 6**. Let's restore these often distorted interpretations.

> The fruits are; love, joy, peace, patience, kindness, goodness, faithful, gentleness, and self control.

LOVE ~ There are three words in Greek that distinguish the different types of love. Agape is divine, unconditional, and self sacrificing. It protects and trusts and is something practiced when none is given in return. Phileo is often seen between family members or friends. Its product is companionship, a mutual sharing and bonds. Eros is a sexual love for a spouse. All three of these should be present in marriage.

JOY ~ The knowledge that God is there and that Jesus died for us to bear our sins. He opened the gates of heaven for us sinners. This underlying principle that is always there and never taken away gives us our joy. What causes it? Jesus' presence. We cannot have an everlasting joy without loving Him. This is a constant, even if we experience a difficult day.

PEACE ~ An acquired harmony between our body and spirit is achieved by having confidence in God's dominion in our life, knowledge that He will care for and provide us with security, and understanding that His will, will be done in divine time and that He always prevails over evil.

PATIENCE ~ Being slow to anger (makro thumos) and slow to act. Take *time* to think through your feelings. Examine the possible behaviors and their outcomes before acting. Difficult situations develop this, and endurance produces it.

KINDNESS ~ This means showing, doing, and speaking mercy, applying compassion to a situation or person, and eliciting empathy for others.

GOODNESS ~ Defined as nearness to God. **Romans 8:28** says, ". . . we know that in all things God works for the good of those who love Him . . . ." We are put through trials; each one we face is 'good' because it is the way to great blessings. We need to acquire the ability to picture outcomes while going through hardship with God in our life. This is *how* God develops us to receive goodness. Knowing this leads us to be filled with it.

FAITHFUL ~ Loyalty through hard and great times, consistent willingness, and obedience. We obtain this by observing His commandments and carrying out their promises to the best of our abilities, no matter what our attitude. Faithfulness is not to be lead astray. These are characteristics of the reliable, firm, and certain person. If we are not full of faith, we will feel insecurity.

GENTLENESS ~ A feeling of security so we may act without harm but with power, not a shout or scream but a firm, loving command. In gentleness we are able to act in confidence, examining the situation or person with respect and tenderness.

SELF CONTROL ~ A choice to delay or restrain an urge caused by an emotional impulse. Call on God to be your support structure. Allow Him to absorb the excess feelings. His strength is far greater than the desire sin puts on us to go against His will.

> Are you beginning to see why we are here on earth?
> Each one of these fruits builds the beauty of your soul.

How do we acquire and keep these in our repertoire?

1. Observe the behaviors of others. Surround yourself with people who display the fruits. Be careful not to compare yourself to someone else.

2. Practice the fruits in daily situations. Begin by planning them into your routine. For example, if your neighbor tends to his lawn every evening at 5 p.m. when you arrive home from work, do you wave and say hello or directly head for the house? Remind yourself by carrying a list of these in your pocket or purse. Place one in your car and make it visible. Post it on the bathroom mirror until they begin to come naturally. Try one or two fruits at a time.

3. Make a list of the undesirable behaviors you tend to exhibit. It is time to be honest. Now, combat each one by writing next to it the opposite behavior and practice it. List specific ways: when, where, how, who, *and* why. This is another way we can achieve

happiness and *fulfill* the fruits so we may *receive* the gifts and be worthy of them.

4. Do not become dissuaded. Master them one at a time and know our God is there to catch us when we fall. Actively turn away from sin and sinful behaviors. God gave us the choice. If you want to be in a happier place in the future, you need to start with the present.

5. Petition in prayer.

6. Keep an eye on temptation. It likes to wait around the corner and pounce when we least expect it. We must anticipate the bait and move past it.

Gifts of the Spirit

> "There are different kinds of gifts, but the same Spirit. There are different kinds of service, but the same Lord. There are different kinds of working, but the same God works all of them in men."
> **1 Corinthians 12:4**

Who? Everyone.
Why? For the common good, working together with our different gifts as one body. '…so that the body of Christ may be built up until we all reach unity in the faith and in the knowledge of the Son of God and become mature, attaining to the whole measure of the fullness of Christ.' **Ephesians 4:12-13**.
When? Given for one's life time or for a situation.
How are they given? As God determines by the Holy Spirit.

1. You will need a notebook or journal and pencil. Draw a line down the middle of the page. Title the first column "Internal Strengths." Title the second column "External strengths." The first one is what values you have within. The second is how you are able to assist others and positively affect the world around you.

2. Ask friends and/or family members to list positive characteristics they see in you without them looking at the list you previously created. Offer to do this for them as well.

3. Do you identify a pattern with how you view yourself and how others perceive you? Circle those that are similar.

4. Read the spiritual gifts and their explanations below.

One of the following is bestowed upon you, and all hold equal concern. They get stronger the more you practice them. Your life will become exponentially fuller.

WISDOM ~ Some people try to 'simplify' their lives. Life is not simple. If it were, we wouldn't learn anything because it takes action and work to seek this trait and diligence to keep it. Listen to God, accept His **words and commands** (repeated many times in the Bible), and apply understanding. Wisdom will enter you and bring abundance. God is most wise. Practice sound judgment and discernment, and this will result in feelings of safety and sweet dreams. Want a good night's rest? Go after wisdom.

God guides us with this. He holds a secret wisdom that he reveals by His spirit. **1 Corinthians 2:6-8**, "…speak a message of wisdom among the mature, but not the wisdom of this age or of the rulers…we speak of God's secret wisdom, a wisdom that has been hidden and that God destined for our glory before time began. None of the rulers of this age understood it, for if they had, they would not have crucified the Lord of glory."
1 Corinthians 2:10 tells us that "…The Spirit searches all things, even the deep things of God." **Verses 12–13** adds, "We have not received the spirit of the world but the Spirit who is from God, that we may understand what God has freely given us. This is what we speak, not in words taught by human wisdom but in words taught by the Spirit, expressing spiritual truths in spiritual words."

KNOWLEDGE ~ A fear of the Lord is the beginning of this attribute. It is imperative to point out that fear means respect, admiration, and appreciation, not to be afraid of Him. This leads us to praise and worship Him. It is referenced in the Bible that "to know" is a form of a relationship. His word results in knowledge, so it should be our desire to seek His truths in scripture.

1 Timothy 6:20-21 tells us to "Turn away from godless chatter and the opposing ideas of what is falsely called knowledge, which some have professed and is so doing have wandered from the faith," and **Galatians 4:9** says, "But now that you know God – or rather are known by God – how is it that you are turning back to those weak and miserable principles? Do you wish to be enslaved by them all over again?"

FAITH ~ I find it interesting how this is a fruit *and* a gift. The gift is through His words and comes by hearing them. The fruit is produced by the Holy Spirit, and activates healing, miracles, and impossibilities. Faith is based on the truth of Christ having been revealed to you.

HEALING ~ This can be given to us by our faithful prayers of His will to be done as He sees fit and by the confession of our sins. The gift of healing includes a multitude of facets, such as social, physical wounds, emotional, spiritual, and psychological disabilities. He may give some people the gift to heal animals and lands to produce life. It is ultimately dependent on how He plans to work through us. God allows this gift through mercy, not out of reciprocity from our prayers. Only Jesus was able to heal every time.

MIRACULOUS POWERS ~ These are given to build up the church body and the work of ministry to bless its members. It occurs first by faith and then by baptism. One may receive a *share* in the miraculous powers in belonging to a church. It takes the whole church, including you.

PROPHESY ~ It is the ability to speak a message from God in a known language. Its purpose is to inform, advise, and counsel. It requires testing to ensure it is backed up by scripture. Prophesy is not the same as being a prophet or foretelling the future.

DISTINGUISHING BETWEEN SPIRITS ~ This is manifested through dreams, visions, or meditation. It is used for encouragement, for those going home to God to help bring about repentance or expose the wicked. It provides an awareness of the spirit of God, essence of a human spirit, angel, or demon. It does not function at will. Care must be taken not to confuse this with the feelings of suspicion. This has nothing to do with physical appearance.

SPEAKING IN TONGUES ~ It is speaking an *unknown* language. It has meaning that someone in the congregation is able to interpret by praying for that ability. The person who speaks in tongues should pray for someone to interpret. If there is not an interpreter, the Bible instructs that they should be quiet. This gift was given to act as a sign to unbelievers.

INTERPRETATION OF TONGUES ~ This gift enlightens and improves the church. If someone speaks in an unknown tongue, pray. If God allows, He will give you the wisdom to interpret their words.

There are several other gifts listed in the Bible that the Lord bestows at His will. Some are service, encouragement, contribution, leadership, and mercy. Specifically, **Romans 12:6-8** lists understanding and counsel.

> "I urge you to live a life worthy of the
> calling you have received."
> **Ephesians 4:1**

> "…since you are eager to have spiritual gifts, try
> to excel in gifts that build up the church."
> **1 Corinthians 14:12**

Lesson Plan Suggestions:

The activities below may be copied for teaching purposes. See the template following this list.

1. **Characters**
a. How does each character employ another?

    b. List each character's strength and weaknesses.

    c. Compare two characters' similarities and differences.

    d. Write an essay examining the dimensions of a character's philosophical, ethical, and aesthetic qualities.

    e. Brainstorm words and phrases to describe each character.

    f. What is accomplished by the Essa's decisions? How does each sign Essa received affect those decisions and relationships?

    g. Describe any connection between your own life and the characters, events, motives, or religious faith.

    h. Each person is given different gifts, according to 1 Corinthians 12. Which gifts does each character have, and how do they help the characters reach their goals and accomplish their purposes?

2. **Themes**
a. List the events of spiritual warfare throughout the novel. What feelings did the character's reveal showing they were on one side or the other?

    b. List the ways God communicates through the novel. Research Biblical passages of how He interacts with us and through us.

3. Significance of setting and elements of setting
a. Draw or construct a model of heaven based on Biblical scripture, paying attention to the five senses. Extra credit: Add something you think may be a part of heaven that is not told.

4. Symbolism
a. Explain what symbolic meaning the following subjects hold: book title, sephirot, signs, Bockman.
   b. What does light represent in this novel? Record a list of vocabulary words used in the novel that describe light.
   c. Distinguish each symbolic part of the Tree of Life and how it relates to religious beliefs.

5. Career research
a. Oceanographer
   b. Botanist
   c. Ecologist
   d. Eco tourist
   e. District attorney

6. Geology
a. What are the characteristics of the national marine monument?
   b. How did the volcanic islands of Hawaii form? Describe their fate.
   c. How can experiencing a new environment affect us? What safety considerations should these characters exhibit when researching the northwest Hawaiian Islands to protect the animal and plant life?
   d. Name each Hawaiian island and what it is known for.
   e. How does Hawaiian culture relate to its environment? State examples.
   f. What gems are used as metaphors in the Bible, and what do they represent?
   g. Define a gyre and describe what it influences in our environment.

7. Flora and fauna

a. Describe the features and function of the following: autograph tree, acacia, monk seal, sea turtle, Laysan albatross, frigate, deep sea angler. Are they indigenous or brought from another place?
b. Describe the interconnectedness of species living in one of the four areas of the monument. Identify the four areas on a map.

8. **Science of chemistry, physics, and biology**
   a. How is each area of science connected to faith and religion?
   b. Write a research paper on a scientific theory hatched within the past five years. How might it affect people if it were proven?
   c. Research and explain the biochemical process of prayer and the brain's reaction.
   d. Summarize the Einstein-Rosen Bridge Theory. What do you find most interesting about it and why?

9. **Ecology**
   a. How could you bring ecological awareness to people in your community? What specific actions and changes could you introduce? Extra credit: Do one of these things.
   b. Write a list of things you can do at school and home to make a positive macro or micro difference on our environment, and provide detailed instructions on how you would go about this.

Lesson plan template for Light between the Leaves

Lesson plan title:

Concept / topic to teach:

Standards addressed:

General goal(s):

Specific objectives:

Required materials:

Anticipatory set (lead-in):

Step-by-step procedures:

Plan for independent practice:

Closure (reflect anticipatory set):

Assessment based on objectives:

Adaptations (for students with learning disabilities):

Extensions (for gifted students):

Possible connections to other subjects:

glossary

Atoll: a circular coral reef or string of coral islands surrounding a lagoon

Archipelago: a large group or chain of islands

Abstract: a condensed version of a piece of writing, a summary

Aerate: to cause air to circulate through

Aphotic: lightless; dark

Buoyancy control vest: a mandatory piece of equipment for scuba diving. It is an expandable bladder, most commonly worn as a vest that can be inflated with air from the tank to increase buoyancy while diving. To decrease buoyancy, it is deflated through a special air-dump valve or hose. It provides positive buoyancy for resting, swimming, or lending assistance to others under water. It also allows maintenance of neutral buoyancy at any depth simply by adding or releasing air.

Carnelian: A semiprecious stone consisting of an orange or orange-red variety

Conceptual model: a diagram that shows of a set of relationships between factors that are believed to impact a target condition

Configuration: the arrangement of parts or elements

Charade: a ridiculous pretense, an absurdly false or pointless act or situation

DAN: Divers Alert Network is a non-profit medical, education, and research organization dedicated to the safety and health of scuba divers

Deciduous: falling off or seasonally shed at a certain stage of development in the life cycle

Decompression stop: A specified time spent at a specific depth for purposes of nitrogen off-gassing; also called a safety stop

Deep sea angler: European and American bottom-dwelling predatory fish. The angler lies on the bottom and lures its prey with a long, wormlike appendage that extends forward and dangles over its mouth. When the lure is touched, the huge mouth opens automatically. The deep-sea angler has luminescent lures and lives at depths of 200 to 600 fathoms. The various species grow from 6 to 40 inches long.

District attorney: an elected official of a county or a designated district with the responsibility for prosecuting crimes. The duties include managing the prosecutor's office, investigating alleged crimes in cooperation with law enforcement, and filing criminal charges or bringing evidence before the grand jury that may lead to an indictment for a crime.

Dive computer: an electronic device used by a scuba diver to measure the dive profile and to display information needed for a safe dive, avoiding decompression sickness. Dive computers address the same problem as decompression tables but perform a continuous calculation of the partial pressure of gases in the body based on the actual dive profile. As the dive computer automatically measures depth and time, it reduces the need for the diver to carry a separate watch and depth gauge and is able to warn of excessive ascent rates and missed decompression stops. Many dive computers also provide additional information to the diver, such as the water temperature or the pressure of the remaining breathing gas in the diving cylinder.

Exotic matter: A hypothetical kind of matter that has both a negative energy density and a negative pressure or tension that exceeds the energy density. All known forms of matter have positive energy density and pressures or tensions that are always less than the energy density in magnitude. In a stretched rubber band, for example, the energy density is 100 trillion times greater than the tension. A possible source of exotic matter lies in the behavior of certain vacuum states in quantum field theory (see Casimir Effect). If such matter exists, or could be created, it might make possible schemes for faster-than-light travel, such as stable wormholes and the Alcubierre warp drive.

Frigate: a large black seabird with powerful wings, a forked tail, and a long hooked beak. Frigates often take food from other birds in flight and are native to tropical waters.

General relativity: a physics theory, formulated essentially by Albert Einstein, that all motion must be defined relative to a frame of reference and that space and time are relative, rather than absolute concepts. Two theories developed by Einstein include the special theory of relativity, which requires that the laws of physics shall be the same as seen by any two different observers in uniform relative motion, and the general theory of relativity, which considers observers with relative acceleration and leads to a theory of gravitation

Grant: a gift, as of land or money, for a particular purpose

Gyre: in oceanography, a ring-like system of ocean currents rotating clockwise in the Northern Hemisphere and counterclockwise in the Southern Hemisphere

Jasper: an opaque cryptocrystalline quartz of several colors

Joan of Arc: French heroine and military leader inspired by religious visions to organize French resistance to the English and to have Charles VII crowned king. She was later tried for heresy and burned at the stake (1412–1431).

Laysan albatross: a large sea bird that ranges across the north Pacific. Its main breeding colonies are in the Hawaiian Islands

Legislation: the power and function of making rules

Monk seal: an endangered, earless seal that is endemic to the Hawaiian Islands; known to the native Hawaiians as Ilio-holo-i-ka-uaua, or 'dog that runs in rough water'

NAUI: National Association of Underwater Instructors, a nonprofit diver training organization

Near-death experience: observations of people who have been close to clinical death or have recovered after having been declared dead. Many claim to have witnessed similar episodes of passing through a tunnel toward a bright light and encountering people who had preceded them in death.

Neoprene: a synthetic rubber produced by polymerization of chloroprene and used in weather-resistant products, adhesives, shoe soles, sportswear, paints, and rocket fuels

NOAA: National Oceanic and Atmospheric Administration, a federal agency focused on the condition of the oceans and the atmosphere

Papahanaumokuakea Marine National Monument: the largest marine conservation area in the United States. It is located in Hawaii and was created by presidential proclamation on June 15, 2006.

Phosphorescent: relating to a type of light that glows softly in the dark and that does not produce heat

Photophore: a light emitting organ

Polychromatic: showing a variety or a change of colors

Predilection: a tendency to think favorably of something in particular; partiality; preference

Proliferate: to grow and produce in rapid speed, as in budding, cell division, or procreation

PSI: Pounds per Square Inch, the common unit of measurement for pressure.
It can be understood as the amount of force that is exerted on an area of one square inch.
Normal atmospheric pressure at sea level is 14.7 PSI.

Recreational diver certification: certification allowing one to dive no deeper than 130 feet

Regulator: a pressure regulator used in a scuba set that supplies the diver with breathing gas at ambient pressure from one or more diving cylinders. The gas may be air or one of a variety of specially blended breathing gases. A gas pressure regulator has one or more valves in series, which let the gas out of a gas cylinder in a controlled way, lowering air pressure at each stage.

Remnant: remaining fragment or scrap

Rhema: a verse of Scripture that the Holy Spirit brings to our attention with application to a current situation or need for direction. The Holy Spirit illuminates particular scriptures for application that are confirmed in our daily walk with the Lord. Every word of God is inspired, and "all scripture is given by inspiration of God, and is profitable for doctrine, for reproof, for correction, for instruction in righteousness" (2 Timothy 3:16).

Rhetorical: asked merely for the effect with no answer expected.

Shoal: a sandbank or sandbar in shallow water

Spiritual warfare: the cosmic war of good versus evil. Its battles are fought daily between God and Satan, between the Christian church and the world system ruled by our spiritual enemy, and between the Holy Spirit and the lusts of the carnal flesh within every human soul.

Technical diver certification: certification permitting diver to exceed recreational dive limits of 130 feet by using advanced procedures and equipment. This certification allows one to penetrate caves and wrecks.

Trajectory: the curve described by a projectile or rocket in its flight

References

Long, Jeffrey; Long, Jody. 'Current NDERF'. *Near Death Experience Research Foundation*. Jody A. Long Professional Websites. 25 April 2011. Web. 25 April 2011. <http://www.nderf.org>.

'Tree of Life (Biblical)'. *Wikipedia*. Wikimedia Foundation, Inc. 23 April 2011. Web. 25 April 2011. <http://en.wikipedia.org>.

'About Icthus'. *Planet Icthus*. Planet Icthus. n.d. Web. 25 April 2011. <http://www.planeticthus.com>.

George, Samuel Joseph. 'The Einstein-Rosen Bridge'. Krioma.net. n.d. Web. 25 April 2011. <http://www.krioma.net>.

'Wormhole'. The Internet Encyclopedia of Science. n.d. Web. 25 April 2011. <http://www.daviddarling.info>.

'Exotic Matter'. The Internet Encyclopedia of Science. n.d. Web. 25 April 2011. <http://www.daviddarling.info>.

'Casimir'. The Internet Encyclopedia of Science. n.d. Web. 25 April 2011. <http://www.daviddarling.info>.

Papahanaumokuakea Marine National Monument. PMNM Webmaster. 28 July 2010. Web. 25 April 2011. <http://www.papahanaumokuakea.gov>.

Northwest Hawaiian Islands Multi-Agency Education Project. Laboratory of interactive learning technologies at the Universtiy of Hawai'i.Web. 25 April 2011. <hawaiianatolls.org>.

'Northwest Hawaiian Islands'. *Ocean Explorer*. Ocean Explorer

Webmaster. 25 June 2010. Web. 25 April 2011. <http://oceanexplorer.noaa.gov>.

'Protecting Marine Ecosystems'. *Marine Conservation Biological Institute*. n.d. Web. 25 April 2011. <http://www.mcbi.org>.

'Northwest Hawaiian Islands'. *Pacific Islands Benthic Habitat Mapping Center*. School of Ocean and Earth Science and Technology at the University at Hawaii at Manoa. 5 Oct. 2009. Web. 25 April 2011. <http://www.soest.hawaii.edu>.

'Acacia Trees'. *20-20 Site*. n.d. Web. 25 April 2011. <http://www.2020site.org>.

National Geographic: Natural Parks Collection: Hidden Hawaii. Dir. n.a. National Geographic, 2009. DVD.

NIV Couples' Devotional Bible. Grand Rapids. Zondervan, 2000. Print.

CPSIA information can be obtained
at www.ICGtesting.com
Printed in the USA
FSHW010409230821
84229FS